Kate had to know more . . .

"Boy, Allegra, you weren't kidding about your sailing ability. You're really great on a boat."

"Thanks. I told you guys I was a different person out here."

You sure are, Kate thought to herself. So different it makes me suspicious. She looked at Allegra, smiling to cover up the fact that she was examining her face. What was it about her that was bugging Kate so much, besides how attractive she'd become?

I know, Kate thought. *It's her eyes. They're darting around all over the place, from the horizon, to Justin, to the back of the boat, to the sky, back to the horizon. It's as if she's looking for something, making mental notes, trying to figure something out. She's got some plans that she's not telling us.*

Look for these titles in the **Ocean City** series:

Ocean City
Love Shack
Fireworks
Boardwalk
Ocean City Reunion
Heat Wave
Bonfire
Swept Away
Shipwrecked*
Beach Party*

And don't miss

BOYFRIENDS GIRLFRIENDS

Katherine Applegate's romantic new series!

#1 Zoey Fools Around
#2 Jake Finds Out
#3 Nina Won't Tell
#4 Ben's In Love
#5 Claire Gets Caught
#6 What Zoey Saw
#7 Lucas Gets Hurt
#8 Aisha Goes Wild

*coming soon

ATTENTION: ORGANIZATIONS AND CORPORATIONS

Most HarperPaperbacks are available at special quantity discounts for bulk purchases for sales promotions, premiums, or fund-raising. For information, please call or write:
Special Markets Department, HarperCollins Publishers, 10 East 53rd Street, New York, N.Y. 10022
Telephone: (212) 207-7528. Fax: (212) 207-7222.

SWEPT AWAY

Katherine Applegate

HarperPaperbacks
A Division of HarperCollins*Publishers*

If you purchased this book without a cover, you should be aware that this book is stolen property. It was reported as "unsold and destroyed" to the publisher and neither the author nor the publisher has received any payment for this "stripped book."

This is a work of fiction. The characters, incidents, and dialogues are products of the author's imagination and are not to be construed as real. Any resemblance to actual events or persons, living or dead, is entirely coincidental.

HarperPaperbacks *A Division of* HarperCollins*Publishers*
10 East 53rd Street, New York, N.Y. 10022

Copyright © 1995 by Daniel Weiss Associates, Inc., and Katherine Applegate
Cover art copyright © 1995 Daniel Weiss Associates, Inc.

All rights reserved. No part of this book may be used or reproduced in any manner whatsoever without written permission of the publisher, except in the case of brief quotations embodied in critical articles and reviews. For information address Daniel Weiss Associates, Inc., 33 West 17th Street, New York, New York 10011.

First printing: April 1995

Printed in the United States of America

HarperPaperbacks and colophon are trademarks of HarperCollins*Publishers*

❖ 10 9 8 7 6 5 4 3 2 1

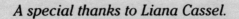

A special thanks to Liana Cassel.

ONE

"Okay, sailor, up and at 'em! Big day ahead and we've got lots of ocean to cover."

Kate Quinn groaned and snuggled farther down into the blankets. The bed shifted slowly beneath her, back and forth, rocking her to sleep. Such a wonderful feeling, she thought. She hadn't slept this well since tenth grade when she'd spent the night at Beth Miller's house and slept in her water bed.

"First mate, Kate Quinn, report for duty!"

She felt the bed dip a bit as Justin sat down beside her. He leaned over and nuzzled her neck, tickling her. "Hey, honey, I love you, but it's time to get up and swab the decks."

"Can't I sleep just a little while longer?"

"What's wrong, Kate?" Justin asked with a laugh. "Jet lag?"

1

Kate opened one eye, and the first thing she saw was a small round porthole of the deepest blue sky imaginable, bobbing in and out of vision. She opened the other eye and smiled. Justin Garrett. The man of her dreams.

Justin smiled and moved forward, dropping down next to her. Kate started to sit up, but Justin put his arms out and stopped her.

"Slowly, slowly." He grinned. "Don't bang your head."

Kate looked up and saw the ceiling an inch above her nose.

"Low roof," she muttered.

"Small boat," Justin corrected. "That means small cabin. And small bed."

"Not too small." Kate sighed happily, remembering the night before.

"Nope," Justin agreed. "Not too small. I was thinking of you when I fixed it up in here, even though I was sure that I'd have this little tiny bed all to myself."

Kate reached out and pulled Justin down to her, nestling into the circle of his arm, her head on his chest.

"You'd never have had it to yourself. Mooch would have kept you company," Kate teased, referring to the shaggy mutt who was probably keeping guard on deck that very moment, sleeping in the shade and snoring loudly.

"It wouldn't have been the same," Justin said.

"I guess not," Kate said. "But I didn't think I'd be here either, until I was actually on the plane."

And she'd gotten there just in time, she realized. One more day and she would have missed him. Kate couldn't help but smile remembering her arrival the day before, and the look of surprise on Justin's face. He'd actually been pushing his boat away from the dock when she'd called out to him. He'd looked up just in time to see her bag flying right at his face. A second after the bag hit the deck, Kate was midair, and then in Justin's arms again. She'd practically knocked them both over.

Kate lifted her head onto her hand and looked deeply into Justin's green eyes. "We didn't really get a chance to talk last night."

"We had other things to catch up on." Justin smiled, caressing her bare shoulder.

"True," Kate agreed, "but I didn't get a chance to say that you were right all along when you told me back in Ocean City that I should come here with you. I was too stubborn to see it."

"No." Justin shook his head. "You had a good plan, Kate, and I just wanted to shake it up. I wanted to be first in your life, before a good summer job and college and all your mapped-out plans for the future."

"Well, you were right to try to shake things

up," Kate said. "Knowing that I was doing the responsible thing wasn't enough to make me feel any better after you left O.C. And now I'm here with you. On your boat." Kate laughed. "And in the Bahamas, of all places! This is paradise, and I almost let it slip through my fingers."

"And it's only for the rest of the summer," Justin reminded her. "We'll be back in O.C. just in time for you to start your sophomore year."

"Let's not think about that now," Kate said, putting her finger on Justin's lips. "I think the jet lag's passing. I feel a burst of sudden energy. Was I dreaming before, or did you say you had a duty assignment for me?"

Justin nodded. "You're to report to the captain's quarters right away."

"What do you suppose he wants?" Kate mused, rolling herself onto Justin's chest, her hands on either side of his head.

"I really couldn't say," Justin whispered, pulling her head down so her lips were just touching his. "Perhaps a discussion of the bilge pump?"

"The bilge pump?" Kate repeated. "What's that?"

"Oh, it's very, very important. Pay close attention."

"Aye, aye, sir," Kate whispered, lowering her mouth.

*   *   *

"Watch out for the boom, Kate!" Justin called out later. "I'm bringing her around."

"Boom. Bringing her around," Kate murmured to herself, trying to get the lingo straight in her head. "Right."

"Duck!" Justin cried.

"Duck? Oh, *duck!* Right," Kate said, lowering her head just in time as the boom swept by.

She looked back sheepishly in Justin's direction, where she could see him shaking his head.

They'd gotten kind of a late start. In fact, they'd missed the entire morning. But now they were out on what Justin called a little "shakedown" cruise—just to check out the boat in preparation for the big sail back to Ocean City.

He's probably wondering if I'm trustworthy as a first mate, Kate thought. *I'm wondering that myself.*

She sighed and looked around. It was silly to be nervous, really, she knew, trying to quell the flip-flopping of her stomach. The whole adventure was like a fairy tale. They were in the Bahamas, after all. What could possibly go wrong there?

The water below them was as clear and turquoise as a pool. Even out there she could see the pale, sandy bottom and the schools of weirdly shaped tropical fish. And she could see the island and the harbor and the marina behind them—the unreal white beaches stretching away on either side, palm trees swaying in the breeze, the thatch of the native islanders' huts, the long, narrow fishing boats lined up on shore. And in the distance she could make out the towers of the luxury hotels in downtown Nassau.

Kate turned her back on town and pretended the island was long gone. They were just far enough out on the boat to be able to see the sun as it began its descent into the deep blue of open water. The colors were gorgeous. The sky was candy-striped from top to bottom, passing through all the shades of the rainbow. It was as if she'd never actually seen real nature, the real sky—until now.

Kate glanced back at the island and thought that it would probably be different to be in the middle of the ocean, where the only thing in sight in any direction would be water. *Even more beautiful, probably,* she thought. But the nagging, paranoid part of her brain wouldn't let her alone: *Beautiful, yes,* it said. *But deadly. Remember what happened to Justin.*

"But he's fine now," Kate said to herself. "Just practice keeping your directions straight. Let's see, port—left. Starboard—right. Bow—front. Stern—back."

Don't worry so much, Kate thought. Sure,

she had a lot to learn about sailing, but she'd be alone with Justin, no other living being around for hundreds, maybe thousands, of miles: the soft sound of the ocean slapping the hull, the salty air—and that cozy little cabin downstairs. The bed was only about the size of a small door, but it served its purpose.

Anyway, Justin had suggested a little splurge before they left—a few days in a luxury hotel. They would have a house-sized bathroom, big refrigerator, and thousand-inch-screen TV. Not to mention a king-size bed and soft cotton sheets.

Kate took a deep breath of the warm, salty air. Suddenly the boat shifted and she slid off her seat, landing hard on the deck.

"Did you do that on purpose?" she cried. But when she looked over at Justin, she could see he hadn't. His forehead was creased with worry lines, and he was frowning.

"Is something wrong?" she asked, getting up.

"I don't know," he said as Kate stepped carefully around the boom to stand next to him at the wheel. "There shouldn't be anything wrong, but *Kate's* handling funny."

Kate smiled, still finding it somewhat strange when Justin talked about his boat as if it were a woman. Kate knew that almost all sailors did that, but this boat had her name.

"It almost feels like she's been tampered

7

with or something. She's not handling the way she did before the storm."

"Well, is that really a surprise? It was a terrible storm. There's bound to be something wrong with the boat."

"That's just it," Justin said slowly. "I figured something would be different, considering the storm and all the months she's been stranded here since Grace left her. But the weird thing is that there isn't anything wrong. She's actually sailing better. It's why I can't sail her quite yet. I'm making allowances for the way she used to sail, and she's a better boat than the one I started with."

Kate looked around them at the deep blue water and shivered. She didn't want to be reminded of why they were down there, retrieving Justin's boat, but water in every direction was making it hard. She didn't want to remember the storm Grace had told her about, the one that had swept Justin off the deck and into the ocean. She didn't want to think of the funeral service they'd held back in O.C., the months of believing Justin was dead and never coming back. She didn't want to consider again the one-in-a-million odds that had led a passing boat to pluck Justin's storm-battered body from the ocean. She shook her head to chase away the memories.

"And here I thought I was getting seasick because the water was rough, when all this time it's because you're not used to your boat sailing so well?" Kate teased.

"Are you really feeling queasy?" Justin asked, peering at her face.

"A little," Kate admitted. "But it'll go away, won't it? All I need is my sea legs, right?"

"Sure. You'll get used to it. Think you can sweat it out for now?"

Kate nodded.

"Good," Justin said, "because I'm not ready to take her in just yet. I want to take a quick look underneath." Justin turned the wheel and began steering the boat back toward the harbor.

"Will you have to take it out of the water?" Kate asked.

"No," Justin replied, "I'll just jump over the side and take a look."

When they reached the marina, Justin dropped anchor and the boat sat rocking slightly in the water.

"You're captain till I get back," Justin said, leaning over and giving Kate a kiss.

"Okay, but I won't go down with the ship."

"See you in a minute," Justin said, and the next thing she knew, he'd stepped off the side of the boat and dropped into the water.

Kate looked around. The sky was just starting

to turn pink and orange. The sails of the other boats in the marina caught the light and blazed like beacons. She could see paper lanterns strung up around the small huts on the beach, and a fire farther away. Shadows moved back and forth in front of the fire, making the light flicker, and drum sounds drifted to her over the water. She watched a group of fishermen sitting in a circle by the boathouse, a pile of nets at their feet. They were going through the nets checking for tears and holes, which they'd retie or patch. Small brown children ran in circles around each other, running under boats that were hung up to be fixed, hiding behind barrels, leaping over crates. They looked like a flock of birds going from tree to tree.

Suddenly a wet hand grabbed her foot, and Kate shrieked.

"Justin!" she screeched, looking down into the water to see his wet hair dark against his scalp, an enormous grin on his face.

"Sorry," he said. "Don't you know you should be careful about hanging over the side of a boat? Haven't you ever seen *Jaws*?"

"Sure," Kate said, snatching her feet back onto the boat. "But if the shark had been half as cute as you, those women would have been screaming and running *into* the water."

Justin swam up beside the boat and pulled

himself over the side. He stood next to her and shook his head, covering her with drops of water. As always, Kate marveled at his lean, muscled body, the deep tan that hours in the sun lifeguarding and working on his boat had given him.

"Who taught you that trick? Mooch?"

"Nope," Justin corrected. "He learned it from me."

"So how's the boat?"

Instantly Justin's face clouded over and his frown returned.

"Well, I knew something was different. It may be a while since I've sailed her, but it just hasn't felt the same. It looks like something's been done to the keel."

"Isn't that the thing that keeps the boat from tipping over?" Kate asked nervously.

"Yeah." Justin nodded. "But don't look so afraid. It's not going to fall off, it's just been worked on. It actually cuts the water better. In fact," Justin sighed, looking away for a minute, "it's the kind of work a real expert would do. Expensive work."

Justin shook his head, and Kate shivered. Somehow what Justin said sounded ominous.

"So what are you saying?"

"What I'm saying, Kate," Justin replied as he walked over to the anchor and started cranking

11

it up, "is that I was afraid my boat would be strung up in some warehouse in need of major repairs. But when I got here, she was sitting in the water, pretty as you please, with just a bit of surface stuff to fix, things broken off or knocked down in the storm—not nearly as bad as I'd been expecting. And nobody said anything about her being out of the water. And they certainly didn't mention anything about her being worked on."

"So you think someone was working on your boat?" Kate asked. "Who would have done that?"

"I don't know," Justin said, his mouth a thin line. "But I think we'd better find out before we take her anywhere."

"I know nothing about that boat," the dock-worker said politely, scratching his head and looking away.

Justin sighed. "I just want to know if it was out of the water."

The man squinted and looked around him. Then he shook his head.

"I am knowing nothing. That is what he tells me."

"Who tells you that?" Kate asked quickly.

"No, no." The man shook his head. "I get in trouble now."

"You won't get in trouble. I promise I won't

say anything," Justin said softly. "Please just tell me what happened. The boat was damaged. So somebody fixed it, right?"

"It's okay," Kate said earnestly, catching the man's eye and smiling. "We really don't want trouble."

The man paused for a minute, then sighed, looking at Kate. "Fix it," he said softly. "Yes. Yes. Someone fix it."

"The keel?" Kate asked. "It was damaged?"

"Keel, yes," the man said. "A good keel now, though, yes? Very good, I think." He scratched his neck and began pulling on the top of the long rubber boot he was wearing.

"Who fixed it?" Justin asked quickly.

A shadow crossed the dockworker's face.

"Do you know who it was?" Kate asked gently. "We would very much like to thank them. That's all."

"You the man wash over the boat, right?" The dockworker looked at Justin. "And the other pretty woman, not this one," the man said, gesturing to Kate, "she bring the boat here and go away."

"Grace." Justin nodded.

"Grace," the man said. "Yes. She say you die in the sea, and we hear nothing. I know a good man, he know this story also, everyone know the story, and he give money to fix the boat. We don't know who will come, but he fix the boat just in case, for the family of you or Grace."

"It was very nice, and we want to thank him," Kate said, putting her hand on the man's sleeve.

"Thank him only?"

"Absolutely. Yes." Kate nodded. "Thank him only."

"The man is Chernak. You can find him. Chernak. Everyone know. He lives here, but he is like you. Not from here."

"Chernak," Justin repeated slowly.

"But he don't want you to know his name," the man explained quickly. "Just a gift, he said, and no name for you. Now if you will tell him I say this, things may go badly for me."

"We won't say anything," Justin promised. "No one will know we talked to you."

"You think," the dockworker said sadly, looking around. "But all know already. All know. They see." He turned his back and trotted away into the fading light.

"That was weird," Kate said. "He seemed almost afraid."

Justin nodded thoughtfully. "If it's just a gift, why all the cloak-and-dagger stuff?"

"I don't know. Sometimes these wealthy philanthropic types are real hermits. They don't like anyone to make a big deal out of what they do. They just like to give, and they're uncomfortable getting too much attention for it," Kate speculated.

"Maybe," Justin said softly, taking her arm. "But I still think we should find this Chernak guy ourselves. I'd like to offer my thanks." Justin's voice was oddly tight. "In person."

TWO

"Connor!"

"Oh, good, yes," Connor Riordan said in his singsong Irish lilt to the reflection of his face in the darkened PC screen. "This is just what I need today. A good, old-fashioned American tongue-lashing."

He straightened in his office chair and ran his fingers through his long, reddish-brown hair. When his boss, the editor in chief of the *Daily Mariner,* Ocean City's local paper, roared like that, it generally meant trouble, usually in the category of "big."

"Okay, what did I do now?" he said under his breath. He looked around the office. "Let's see, my steamy investigative gem on the multiple uses of suntan oil was too sordid for Ocean City's Family Values Association. Or, oh yes, quite—must be that my feature on the best crab salad in town caused a stampede on Ricky's Clam Bar."

Connor had spent most of the afternoon bouncing the eraser end of his pencil off the screen in front of him. Listening to the distant roll and thunder of Ocean City's famous surf, thinking of all the rich novel material in his brain evaporating by the minute, he reminded himself that every writer of great literature has to pay his dues. They all start as nobodies, he told himself. Nobodies chained to the desk of a newsless newspaper crafting simpleton prose for the high-literati crowd of muscle-heads and beach bunnies. At last count his most ambitious sentence consisted of twelve whole words, four of which had been cut by the copy editor. He yearned to reel off those wild paragraphs, those serpentine sentences, and that flaming Irish dialogue.

The last few weeks he'd managed to get partway through a new novel and had sent out some chapters to a few agents and editors. But he'd heard nothing. Not a peep. Not even a photocopied fill-in-the-blank rejection letter: *"Dear Writer: Thank you for giving us the opportunity to read your manuscript. Unfortunately, this fine work does not suit our current needs. Please do not hesitate to send us anything in the future. In the meantime, good luck placing this work else-where. The editors."*

In the meantime . . . in the meantime. In the meantime he had to eat, he had to make a living. So here he was, dragging his feet across the office.

"Connor!" the voice growled in the next room.

"Yes, boss man," Connor said. "Coming."

Connor leaned his thin frame against the doorjamb and faced his boss's desk. Mr. Hopkins, a wealthy, deeply tanned ex–New Yorker who'd retired early and moved to Ocean City, starting up the paper to occupy his days of leisure, seemed surprised at the sight.

"You look sick. What's wrong with your hair?" Mr. Hopkins asked, his eyes narrowing.

"Luck of the Irish," Connor said, smiling gingerly. "Strawlike hair that stands on end on command without the assistance of either mousse or spray. Quite an achievement, really. One of our best, second only to our fair skin, which can singe and flake away under the heat of a desk lamp in a matter of minutes. And the unmatched diversity of our potato recipes."

His boss looked up, openmouthed, then shook his head.

"Right. Sit down, Riordan," he commanded. "And try to listen to what I'm saying here."

"Always," Connor said, his brow knitted seriously. "Always take my job seriously . . ."

"Quiet! You see? That's just what I mean. Look, we're not exactly a high-pressure operation here, are we?"

"Well, I wouldn't say that," Connor said, folding his arms and knitting his brow. "Our role in Ocean City is no doubt indispensable. After all, where else would one go to find coupons for free flip-flops and scathing editorials about the suggested rule changes for beach volleyball? One must keep things in perspective, boss. For instance—"

"Enough!" Mr. Hopkins yelled. He slid yesterday's edition across his desk toward Connor. The paper was peeled back to the obituary page. Connor beamed with pride. There was his obituary of Richard Adelman, a prominent businessman, largely responsible for Ocean City's recent boom, who had died the week before. Adelman was one of the paper's biggest advertisers. Mr. Hopkins had instructed Connor to give the obit a real glow, to bask Mr. Adelman's memory in the glory of his achievements. It was the first assignment Connor had taken to heart. He hadn't known Adelman, but hey, the guy had died. He did his novelist's best to pay his respects.

Mr. Hopkins's index finger came to rest on the photo accompanying the obituary.

"Who's this, Connor?"

"Uh, let me guess. Richard Adelman?"

"That's right," Mr. Hopkins said, folding his arms across his chest. His face went tomato-red as he glared across the desk at Connor.

"Did Mr. Adelman's family not like the obituary or something?" Connor asked, puzzled by Mr. Hopkins's apparent anger.

"No, Connor. They were quite impressed. In fact, I got a call from Richard Adelman himself this morning expressing his gratitude at the way the paper portrayed him."

"Wonderful!" Connor said, feeling a momentary pang of self-satisfaction. "But . . . but wait. What do you mean Richard Adelman called you this morning? That's his obit. The man's dead!"

Mr. Hopkins smiled self-righteously. "Well, that's the point, Connor, ol' boy. Richard Adelman isn't dead. You wrote the wrong obit. You killed off one of Ocean City's most influential people."

"But I . . ." Connor sputtered. "You told me . . . you wrote down the name . . . I don't get it."

"Adel*son*, Connor. Robert Adel*son*."

Connor opened his mouth to say something, but all that came out was breath.

"Exactly," Mr. Hopkins said. "All I can say is that I hope for your sake Mr. Adelman doesn't stop advertising with us. Because if he does, we may have to make some staff adjustments around here." Mr. Hopkins looked at Connor with a you-know-what-I'm-getting-at look. "I have a meeting with him tomorrow afternoon."

"Well, I mean the man has a sense of humor, doesn't he?" Connor said.

"Out," Mr. Hopkins said, raising his arm toward the door.

"Adelson, Adelman, you can see how I mixed it up, can't you?"

"Out!"

Chelsea dropped her jacket onto the sofa, went straight for the fridge, popped open a diet Coke, and made for the little balcony off the living room. By now it had become an old routine since she'd given up her job drawing beach-scene portraits of snot-nosed, hyper kids for their sunburned, overly demanding parents and taken a job in an air-conditioned office, doing graphic art for a small local advertising company. At five on the button she dropped whatever she was working on, headed for the door, and for home.

Usually she got there before Connor and was able to steal a few minutes of privacy, admiring the sunset, catching her breath. Life seemed to be moving so quickly. Here she was, twenty, already making a living with her art and already married. Only a few months ago she'd been sure it was going to take years to get to this place.

The sky above her had just begun to redden with early evening. She leaned around the corner of the building to enjoy the apartment's "water view": across the street, through the trees, over the beach—a narrow strip of dark blue ocean. The horizon was almost indigo and bled upward shades of ever-lighter reds and oranges.

The lap of luxury, she thought sarcastically. Then she stood up straight and, leaning her back against the house, propped her feet on the railing and downed the rest of her soda.

What am I complaining about? she wondered. *Just a few weeks ago I was separated from my husband and willing to do anything to be an artist, even if it meant waiting tables and living in a hovel. But look at me, back in my apartment with a man who loves me, and a steady income. Make that two steady incomes,* she thought, remembering Connor's job at the local paper.

Ahh, Connor, Chelsea thought happily. For the first time in months their relationship was actually traveling along on a smooth track. First there were all the initial questions: the should-we-or-should-we-not-get-married, the can-we-or-can-we-not-deal-with-the-racial-differences, and the do-I-love-him-or-am-I-marrying-him-so-he-can-become-a-U.S.-citizen question.

Then when they'd finally decided just to do it,

they'd moved to New York, where they'd tried, and failed, living together as artists. Chelsea had had school, at least, but Connor had had nothing. Just a menial job at McDonald's while he'd tried to write in their tiny apartment. Pretty soon the fact that her parents were supporting them had started to affect them both, and they'd bickered and fought constantly.

And when they came back to O.C. to try to work things out, instead of getting better, everything had unraveled. She'd even moved across the street into Grace's house, and they'd both tried to live the lives of independent—and unmarried—people.

Fortunately, her boss, Paul Hagen, had hired her and Connor for the same ad campaign. If they hadn't had to spend so much time working together, they might never have spoken again. And they might never have realized how much they really loved each other.

The portable phone in the living room started to chirp, interrupting Chelsea's memories.

"Hello?" she said, cradling the phone on her shoulder.

"Chelsea?"

"Oh, hi, Mom," Chelsea said, sinking back into the sofa cushions and propping her feet up on the coffee table. "What's up?"

"We-ell," her mom said, as if she were bursting

with news. "Nothing much. Just that your cousin had her baby last night!"

Chelsea sat up excitedly. "Really? Ohmygod. Marissa had her baby? What is it, a boy or a girl?"

"A girl. But that's not the good part."

"Not the good part! What could be better than another female in this family to help outweigh all those muscle-head boys?"

"Why don't I let Marissa tell you herself?" her mother said.

"She's back from the hospital already?" Chelsea cried into the phone.

"You bet I am." Marissa's voice came onto the line.

"Marissa! I can't believe it. You're a mom! I still think of you as that little punk who pulled my hair and mixed up all my art pencils and told my mother the first time I kissed a boy."

"I still am all those things, cuz," Marissa said. "But now I have a little assistant to torment you through adulthood."

Chelsea whistled into the phone. "I still can't believe it. We're growing up so fast."

"Better believe it, Chels. Life's whipping right by. Me a mom. You a married woman. We gotta grab life by the ears and wring it for all it's worth."

Chelsea paused. Her cousin seemed tired, different—older, too. More grown-up.

"Chels? You still there?"

"I'm here," Chelsea said. "It's just that . . . I don't know. You sound so different."

"I *am* different, Chels. Life'll never be the same again. I'm a mom. *Forever.*"

Both paused, as if letting that sink in.

"So aren't you even going to ask me what her name is?" Marissa said.

"Oh, yeah, I forgot," Chelsea said.

"Selena," Marissa said. "The sun goddess."

"Selena," Chelsea repeated, trying it out on her tongue. "I like it. Wait. No, I love it. It has dignity."

"So you want to hear the good news, or the *really* good news?" Marissa asked.

"Hm, let me see. I'll take 'good' for a hundred dollars," Chelsea quipped.

"Selena's middle name."

Chelsea sucked in her breath. Did she dare think it?

"What is 'Chelsea'?" she whispered.

"Cor*rect!*" Marissa cried, and both she and Chelsea screamed and giggled.

"Marissa, I can't believe it. I'm so . . . I don't know . . . *honored.* But what's the *really* good news?"

"Well," Marissa began, "godparents, for a hundred dollars."

Chelsea's jaw dropped. "Who are Chelsea and . . . *Connor?*"

25

"Cor*rect!*" Marissa cried again.

"Oh, my God! I don't believe it! I'm so . . . I mean, we're so honored. Connor's so honored he doesn't even know it."

"Well, he better be. It's going to be trouble enough explaining to Selena what a carrot-topped Irishman is doing in our family. But you're coming down for the christening, right?" Marissa asked.

"Of course," Chelsea said. "What's a christening without the godparents?"

"Besides, it'll be a great chance for Connor to stumble into all your old boyfriends. Get his Irish dander up."

"What are you talking about, Marissa? Why would any of my old boyfriends be at Selena's christening?"

"Why, you remember Antonio Palmer, don't you?" Marissa said, her voice laced with multiple meanings.

Chelsea sank back into the couch and gulped involuntarily. "Antonio? Antonio's going to be there?"

"He's coming with B.D. from the naval academy. You knew he was at the academy, didn't you?"

"I heard about that. He went in after his mom died. But I haven't seen Antonio in—I don't know how long," Chelsea said dreamily.

"Uh-oh," Marissa chirped. "Do I hear the sizzle of that old flame still flickering?"

"Marissa!" Chelsea said scoldingly. "I'm a married woman!"

"Of course you are. But there wasn't a young thing in our neighborhood who wasn't watering after that dude. And I've seen him lately. I'm married too, but he's still a mm-mm good-looking son of a gun."

Chelsea laughed. "Come on, Marissa. Let's not get carried away. I mean, I *liked* Antonio and all. We were practically best friends . . . but it was never anything more than platonic."

"Uh-huh," Marissa said again. "Sure, honey. But that's only because you were a Cath-o-lic, with a capital C."

"Marissa!"

"You're right, Chels," Marissa laughed. "The past is the past. We've all got new responsibilities, new lives. I'm a mommy and you're a married woman. We can't be going backward, now, can we?"

"That's right, Marissa. We can't."

"But it doesn't mean we have to go blind either," Marissa shrieked.

"I guess not," Chelsea agreed, suddenly wildly anxious to see Antonio again.

"Are you ready to cool off yet?"

27

Grace could barely hear David's voice as the wind whipped it past her. She was holding him tightly around the waist, her cheek resting on the back of his worn leather jacket, the motorcycle humming below them as David drove along the miles of deserted beach toward the national park north of Ocean City.

It was late afternoon, and the sun was starting to fall over the bay, off to their left, casting long shadows across them and out into the darkening water of the ocean. They were riding over the dunes, cattails flying past on either side, their soft, fuzzy tops catching Grace on the legs as they passed.

David turned the bike toward the ocean, and Grace tightened up. An image flashed through her mind, of her mother, naked with a drink in her hand, heading toward the waves. Again Grace remembered the late-night call: *We'll need you to identify her* . . . She held on tightly to David's waist, feeling his muscles harden and flex as he turned the bike at the last instant and ran it along the edge of the water, kicking up spray behind them.

But she had David, Grace knew. And her mother had had no one. It was a difference she would never let herself forget. David Jacobs had saved her life, Grace thought, as she peeked around the dark curls of his hair to catch a glimpse of his mouth set in a line, a look of concentration on his handsome face. He'd stayed by her when she first went in to A.A. And, a member himself, he'd understood.

He'd let her go with Justin at the end of last summer, knowing how badly she still felt she needed to see more of the world, knowing how she'd needed to leave Ocean City for a while. Then he'd been there when she'd returned, to welcome her back and help her move on after her mother's death, when Grace had found herself in charge of property, a large bank account, and her sixteen-year-old-brother, Bo.

Not to mention how supportive he'd been when Grace had decided to become legal guardian to Roan, the young runaway she'd found on the boardwalk. David had helped her deal with Roan's drug and alcohol problems and with the relationship that had developed between Roan and Bo. And he'd even gone with her down to Macon when Grace had finally decided that the only thing she could do to really help Roan was to make it official—adopt her and give her a real home to live in.

And of course, perhaps the biggest gift of all, David had taught her to fly. Everything with David seemed about flying, even now, on the motorcycle, flying over the dunes, racing the ocean, her hair blowing back from her face.

She closed her eyes, leaned back, and listened to the sound of the motorcycle's engine drowning out the sound of the waves. She smelled the salt air, the wet sand, the engine burning oil. Her fingers held tightly to David's jacket, the leather old and soft. Suddenly she couldn't contain herself and she shrieked with joy.

Instantly David slowed down.

"What! What!" he cried. "Grace? Are you okay?"

She laughed and hugged him tightly.

"Yes, sorry," she said, leaning forward so that he could hear her. "Don't mind me. I was just feeling particularly alive a minute ago."

"Well, next time you feel so alive, do me a favor and warn me before you start screaming with joy. I thought you were hurt."

He turned the bike away from the water and up onto the beach, then came to a stop. The sudden silence around them was almost deafening. They could hear the sound of the ocean again, the water slapping on the wet sand of the beach.

Neither of them moved for a while. Finally Grace unhooked her arms from David's waist and sat back. She sighed and slipped off the bike. David rolled to a spot where the sand was packed solidly and worked the bike onto its kickstand. Then he unhooked the cooler and the blanket he had brought from the back of the bike. He spread the blanket out and began unpacking their dinner.

"Looks like a feast," Grace noted, her eyes sparkling with excitement as David pulled out carefully wrapped packages of grilled shrimp, papaya salad, bread . . .

"I even brought drinks," he said, nodding wisely.

"Drinks?" Grace asked, raising her eyebrow.

David took out a bottle of sparkling water and two plastic stem glasses. "Ta-da," he said. "Well, what do you think?"

Grace surveyed the spread. Then she looked out at the ocean, then back at David.

"It looks awfully tempting, but I thought you said we were going to cool off when we got here," she remarked.

"That run by the water didn't get you wet?" he asked innocently.

"Let's skip the nonsense," Grace said, a smile playing at the corners of her mouth. "Take off your clothes."

"My clothes!" David cried, trying unsuccessfully to look offended. "But what about dinner?"

"It'll keep." Grace smiled. She pulled her shirt off over her head.

"What do you—"

Before he could finish, Grace had shucked off her shorts and was running for the water.

"A swim?"

She could hear David's forlorn cry behind her.

"You're telling me you want to *swim*? You're nasty, do you know that, Grace?"

Grace dived for the water and felt its coolness close around her. She shot out quickly, shrieking, her body covered with goose bumps. She turned to find David at the edge of the waves.

"Come on," she cried. "Get in here while the getting's good."

"It's cold," he said, laughing.

"What's wrong?" Grace taunted. "Can't take it?"

"Is that a challenge?" David asked. "I certainly hope so."

"Sure," Grace replied, her heart starting to beat faster. "If you can catch me."

She dived off to the right and started swimming away, with strong, powerful strokes. But after only a second or two she felt a hand close around her ankle, and she was brought up short, sucked under water for a minute, before being twisted around.

Then she found herself in David's arms.

"Suddenly the water doesn't seem so cold," Grace panted, her lips close to his. "Did you notice that?"

"Was it ever cold?" David said softly, his hands dropping below the waves to take her around the waist.

THREE

Connor stood leaning his head against the partition of his minuscule cubicle. The late-afternoon sun filled the window, sending dust-filled ribbons of light across the room and against the opposite wall like laser beams. What he wanted to do was sit down and write a paragraph about how the tides of light sift like the nearby ocean, in and out of the window. But instead he was faced with a half-baked article about a rash of minor food poisoning caused by underdone crab cakes.

As he sat in his office chair, he noticed that the one sign of life in the office, a plant he'd nurtured from near death, had wilted and lay sprawled and browned across his desk. All he could do was nod.

"Appropriate," he said to himself. "Yup, it's

an omen, all right. I'm not going anywhere."

Just then something caught his eye. There was actually an envelope in his in-box. When he picked it up, he realized it wasn't merely an envelope. It was a manila envelope with his own handwriting on it. He'd included one with each of his submissions to the New York agents and editors. He'd always thought it was a strange ritual: Not only did they bash you with mailed rejections, but they made you pay for the stamp.

Connor didn't breathe. He peered at the envelope as if it were a letter bomb. He held it carefully up to the sunlight. Inside was a letter. Not the small squares of paper that began "Dear Writer". . . . A letter.

"Forget it, Riordan," he said to himself. "You're not going anywhere. This is your life. Overblown obits about forgettable people for a meatball newsletter. Get used to it."

He tore it open with his teeth, dumped the contents into his hands, and began to read. Then he read it again. And again. Then he stood up.

He walked in a straight, unhurried line to Mr. Hopkins's office. He stood in the doorway until Mr. Hopkins raised his head. The man's eyes narrowed with annoyance at the sight of Connor.

"Finished that crabcake article yet, Riordan?"

"No, sir," Connor said evenly.

"The deadline was over an hour ago."

"I believe that's correct."

Mr. Hopkins frowned. "You're walking on thin ice, Connor."

"I think the ice has broken, sir," Connor said with a straight face.

"What are you talking about?" Mr. Hopkins said, his irritation growing by the second.

"I'm talking about my own obituary, Mr. Hopkins."

"What—?"

"My obituary will say, 'Connor Riordan began his professional writing career at a minor daily for an editor of questionable taste and talent. But his tenure there was short-lived. Following minor confusion over a silly little obituary, he told his boss to take his job and, as the saying goes, shove it.'"

"You're fired, Riordan!" Mr. Hopkins crowed.

"I don't think so, Mr. Hopkins. Because I quit!"

Chelsea ducked as a flock of seagulls whooshed by overhead. The birds moved like a cloud toward the beach, banking left and dive-bombing in tightly formed squadrons for their nightly feast of leftovers from the day's tourists.

Chelsea padded along the boardwalk toward Connor's office. The wooden slats, still baking with the heat of the sun, felt good against her bare feet. The beach front was mostly empty. A few young couples strolled by. A man in bright-orange overalls with "O.C. Sanitation" on the back was sweeping up the ice-cream wrappers and soda cans and pizza crusts. The whole boardwalk looked used, tired.

But none of it mattered now. Not with the wonderful news she was bringing to Connor. Godparents. She could still hardly believe it. She knew she was young to be married, and she wasn't ready to start thinking of a family yet, but somewhere her heart was tugging at her. A little baby girl. With her name.

Someday she'd be christening her own baby girl. Now that was an interesting thought. What would her baby look like? Coffee-colored skin with flaming-red hair, or pale and freckled with a frizzy Afro? Chelsea laughed out loud imagining it.

"What's so funny?" said a foreign, lilting voice behind her.

Chelsea whirled around. "Connor!"

Without knowing it she'd walked right by his office and was headed out of town.

"Aye, lassie, Connor's name, and bliss is the game," he sang in his cracked Irish tenor.

Chelsea leapt into his arms. He lifted her chin and pressed his lips against hers. Their marriage was still so young, but his body felt so familiar already. He knew just how to hold her. He knew just how to kiss her.

"Wow," she said, pulling back, her deep black eyes glistening in the twilight.

"Wow what?"

"Some kiss," Chelsea said, puckering her lips.

Connor stepped toward her and wrapped her in his arms again. "And there's more where that came from, lassie. But where might you be going just now? All the way to Philadelphia?"

"I was coming to pick you up at work."

"Aren't you a sweet thing?"

"I have some wonderful news to tell you, but I walked right by your office," Chelsea said, shaking her head.

"You mean, *ex*–office," Connor said.

"Ex—? What? Connor, what are you saying? You quit?"

Connor took Chelsea by the waist and waltzed her badly across the boardwalk, tripping over her feet, off the railing and back the other way, all the while singing a medley of Irish folk songs in her ear.

"Connor, wait," Chelsea panted, laughing, gasping for breath. "What's going on?"

"Wait, she says! You want me to wait?"

Connor stalked up to the sanitation worker and tapped him on the shoulder, startling him out of his working daze. "You see that lovely little morsel over there?" he asked, pointing in Chelsea's direction. "She wants me to wait!"

Chelsea hid her eyes, embarrassed. "Connor!" she cried happily. She felt overwhelming relief. *He's such a lunatic,* she thought. *He's such a lovable, ranting, raving lunatic.*

Connor ran back to Chelsea, leaving the sanitation worker shaking his head. "I wait for no man. Or woman," Connor declared. "A published author waits for nothing!"

"A published what?" Chelsea said, taking a step back as Connor whipped a folded envelope out of his pocket and waved it in the air like a checkered victory flag. Chelsea covered her mouth with her hands. "Connor, no!"

"Connor, yes!" Connor cried. "Yes yes yes yes yes!" He did an awful jig. "Some desperate editor-type in New York has finally taken pity on yours truly, Connor Riordan, previously unpublished, unread, unwritten, and unformed. And now . . . and now . . ."

"And now?" Chelsea asked, her heart galloping with excitement.

Connor took Chelsea in his arms again. "And now whose life has changed forever."

"But how?" she asked, wide-eyed.

The lamps started popping on one at a time up and down the boardwalk, like little suns, giving the twilight a magical quality.

Connor stepped back. "Because a truly wonderful thing just happened, Chelsea."

"What, what?" Chelsea asked excitedly. "Tell me already."

"Be patient, my dear. I want this moment to be the start of forever."

Chelsea peered up into Connor's eyes. He was so romantic. He had a way with words that cut right to her heart. "I love you, Connor," she said. "And I'll love you forever."

Grace felt David's fingers fluttering up and down her spine. The water moved against her as her body melted into a warm, pliable liquid. Then one hand came out of the water and worked its way up her neck and into her hair. David's lips were soft on hers, and Grace couldn't hear anything but the sound of her own heartbeat.

She ran her own fingers along the smooth hardness of his shoulders, again, as always, amazed at how beautiful he was. Grace knew how special David was. Intelligent, honest—

"Not to mention sexy as hell," Grace mouthed against his lips.

"Hmmm," David sighed, his breath warm. "My thought exactly."

Grace leaned back and looked into his dark brown eyes. The sun was really falling below the tree line now, and David's hair was reddish-brown in the glow of the sunset. She sighed deeply.

"I love you, David," she said softly. "So much it almost hurts to look at you."

She smiled, but her smile faltered, because something flickered in David's gaze and he looked away.

"I love you too, Grace," he said softly, pulling her closer as he looked out toward the ocean.

"It sounds like you're about to say 'but,'" Grace said, her heart stopping in her chest.

"It's not a 'but' you won't understand, Grace," he said softly. "There's a reason I brought you out here tonight. There's something I need to tell you."

Instantly Grace felt herself go numb. Instinctively she started to pull away, but David held on to her tightly.

"Hear me out, Grace, please," he said softly in her ear, "before you start pulling away."

But Grace couldn't even feel the water around her anymore. She looked down to see his hands holding her shoulders, but she didn't feel them. And from far away, it seemed, she heard his voice in her ear.

40

"Remember last summer, your trip to New York with Kate and Chelsea? You came home and couldn't stop talking about it, and you had the bug to travel, to see some more of the world."

Grace did remember that long-ago morning, lying in David's bed, the understanding in his eyes. *"Oh, man, you've got it bad,"* he'd said. . . . *"Wanderlust, the hunger for the open road . . ."*

"I knew you needed to leave," David went on softly. "And I knew you were going to leave. Even though you loved me then, too. You didn't want permanence and possession yet," David was saying. Grace tried to concentrate, but the memories kept interrupting.

"There's still a hell of a lot of the world I haven't seen either. . . . I'm not ready for that yet, but the day will come again when I am . . ."

"Remember what I told you?" David asked.

Grace looked at him and nodded, her eyes suddenly filling with tears. She knew then, without his saying any more, that he was leaving. She was going to lose him. And even though she understood, even though she'd done it too, it already hurt. At that moment she realized how it would hurt to be the one left behind. She hadn't had to think about that when she'd gone with Justin. She was too excited about seeing all the things she'd dreamed of.

41

David moved his hands up to her shoulders and stroked them softly as he spoke to her.

"I encouraged you because I knew what you needed to do for yourself. And I also told you that someday I might be ready to do the same thing."

"I remember," Grace whispered.

"I've had an offer, Grace," he said slowly. "I've had similar ones before. But I wasn't ready to take them."

"And you're ready now," she guessed tonelessly.

David nodded. "Not because I'm any less in love with you," he said. "Not because I feel like we've had enough. I don't want you ever to think that. It's because I'm ready. Because I need to do it, and maybe even because I'm more in love with you now than I've ever been."

"What does that mean?" Grace asked breathlessly. "In love enough to leave?"

"Grace, I love you," David said, his fingers tightening on her arms. "But I'm not really happy in O.C. I need more for myself than teaching flying lessons. If I don't get more, it won't matter how much I love you. I'll start to be unhappy. And I don't ever want to blame you for my unhappiness."

Grace shook her head as if maybe she could

shake the words out. "So what's the offer?" she said sadly.

"F-15s," David said softly. "It would mean out of the little Cessna and back into a jet."

As much as she tried not to hear it, Grace couldn't help noticing the sound of his voice, the marveling, the excitement. How could she ever ask him to give that up?

"Doing what?"

"Instructing," David said. "So still a teacher, of sorts. But not in a two-seater. Not anymore. The air force will take me back, for the F-15s, if I want."

Grace knew then that there was more behind all this than just the big jet versus the little plane. More than just a new city. Both those things were important, but this was also something else for David. Something about pride. He'd beaten his drinking, and the air force trusted him again. They wanted him back.

"Where?" Grace's voice was small as she asked, knowing before he spoke that it would have to be somewhere far away, somewhere too far away to believe anything between them could still last.

"Taiwan," David said, the sound of the word breaking Grace's heart.

But she leaned in and hugged him. Held on

for dear life so she wouldn't sink under the water. Let him pick her up and hold her.

"I'm happy for you, David," she whispered into his neck. "Let's celebrate with a toast. I really need a drink. Of that water." She smiled so that he could hear it in her voice, but she kept her face against his neck as he carried her from the ocean, hoping her tears would be lost in the salt water.

"I don't believe it," Chelsea said for the hundredth time. She was holding up the editor's letter to the lamplight. She started to shake.

"How can you read with all that quivering?" Connor asked excitedly. He peered over her shoulder. "Where are you? Have you gotten to the good part yet?"

"Good part? It's all good, Connor. What's not good?"

"How about the part where it says, 'Your novel, *Beach Blanket Begorra,* is a complex and many-layered work'?"

"*Beach Blanket Begorra!*" Chelsea cried. "*Beach Blanket Begorra?*" She began to laugh. "What's a '*begorra'?*"

Connor pointed over her shoulder at the letter. "But see there?"

"Where?"

Connor's index finger stabbed at the page. "There. 'Writer of great promise'? See that?"

"I see that," Chelsea said.

"That's me. I'm the writer of great promise. Now what about 'Your lyrical, bitingly witty prose set the entire editorial staff frolicking out the door to lunch'?"

"I didn't realize you were so funny," Chelsea mused aloud, more to herself than to Connor.

"Thanks a lot, Chels. Thanks for your patronage. Always appreciated. We artists will accept any scrap of support. There. How about 'I hope to have the pleasure of working with you in the very near future, and for some time to come'? How about them apples, as you Yanks always say?"

"Do you have this entire letter memorized?" Chelsea asked.

"Absolutely," Connor said.

Chelsea shook her head and blinked up at Connor. "When did you have time to do all this writing?"

"Well. That's an interesting question. It just so happens that it was while we were separated, having, of course, nothing else to do but stay at home and mope and consider my dreadful life without you in it. I'm always mouthing off about being a writer. I thought I might as well put my money where my mouth was. It started off as a goof. But I

45

wrote the first page and kept going. Between mopes, that is. Moping is good. Moping is inspirational. Moping, I learned, is a writer's best friend."

"Maybe I should leave you again," Chelsea quipped.

Connor took Chelsea by the shoulder. "But moping wasn't any fun."

Chelsea slapped the letter. "But look what happened, Connor! Our marital troubles were a blessing in disguise."

Connor scratched his head. "They were? They don't feel like it."

Chelsea went back to the letter. Her fingers stopped about three fourths of the way down.

"What's that?" Chelsea said. She squinted at the paper and pointed. "What about this part here that says, 'Thank you for these first few chapters. Our interest is genuine, but we cannot make a firm offer until we see the rest, the sooner the better. If you could mail us the remainder of your novel by next week, we'll get in touch with you shortly thereafter.'"

"That," Connor said, suddenly looking a little confused, "is the bad part."

"Why's it the bad part?"

"Because there is no 'rest,'" Connor said.

"Then why would they ask for it?"

"Because they *think* there's a rest," Connor said.

"But why would they think that?"

Connor winced. He looked at Chelsea worriedly. "Because I lied?"

"You lied?"

"Like I said. I was moping. I needed to feel better. So I told myself I'd written the whole novel and was sending out just bits and pieces of it to see if there was interest. I started to believe it myself, that I'd written the whole thing."

"So, okay. No big deal. Just finish it," Chelsea said, blasé, handing back the letter.

"So *okay*? So *finish* it? Just like that?" Connor said, aghast.

"Yeah. *Finish* it. I'll help you if you want."

"You? Help? Just finish it?" Connor walked away a few steps dramatically and started motioning in the air. "But I need ideas. I need material. I need—"

"Me?" she wondered aloud.

"Well, not quite," Connor said, wincing.

"What do you mean *not quite?*"

"Chels, come *on,*" Connor said. "You're an artist. You understand. I mean, writing's not exactly a group activity."

"I guess," she said sadly. "I'll have to get used to it. I just want to be in on everything, you know? It's just weird that something so important to you has nothing to do with me."

Connor put his arm around her shoulder. He

bent down and put his lips next to her ear. "But it does have to do with you," he whispered. "Because something good for me is something good for you. It's good for us. It makes us more of a family."

She turned and looked at Connor, filled with conflicting thoughts. "Well, I'm glad you said that, Connor," she said. "Because Marissa just had her baby."

"Well, jolly good!" Connor said.

"And the baby's middle name is Chelsea!"

Connor was grinning from ear to ear.

"And . . . and . . ."

"There's more?" Connor said.

"She wants us to be her daughter's godparents!"

Connor frowned and whistled. "Gee, Chels," he said, rubbing his temple. "I don't know. It's kind of a lot of responsibility, isn't it? I mean, looking after it if something, you know, happens to Marissa or anything."

"Connor, don't be morbid! It just means that we have to be the *cool* relatives."

"You mean hear its confessions and all that, and take it out and get it drunk for the first time?"

"*It*'s got a name, Connor, and it's Selena."

"Selena. Selena," Connor repeated. "A bit . . . I don't know—far-out, isn't it?"

Chelsea slapped him playfully on his arm.

"I think it's beautiful," she said. "It means 'sun goddess.'"

"Okay, so what exactly *are* our responsibilities?"

"I'm glad you asked, because number one is attending her christening this weekend in D.C."

Connor arched his eyebrows. "This weekend?"

"Yeah, we can take the train, have some fun. Did I ever tell you how much I love trains, Connor?"

"Uh, no, Chels, you never did, but—"

"And you and B.D. can go out and play basketball and do guy things while Marissa and I go shopping for baby stuff."

"Sounds, um, interesting, Chels," Connor stammered. "But I don't know."

"What do you mean you don't know?"

"I mean, I've got to get cracking on this book," Connor said.

"But you can get cracking for the next few days, take the weekend off, then get cracking on it again Monday morning," Chelsea said, her voice rising a little with exasperation.

Connor took Chelsea around the waist. "Let's talk about it later, Chels, okay?" he said cheerfully.

But it wasn't okay. At that moment Chelsea realized that as of tonight nothing was going to be the same. Connor was going to be a published author. What he said about its strengthening them as a family was nice, but she knew it wasn't the whole story. For instance, there was Selena's christening. Yesterday he would have jumped at the chance to get out of O.C. for a weekend. But not now. No, everything was going to change, and change fast. Her intuition told her that she was going to have to hold on for a bumpy ride.

FOUR

Kate and Justin watched the island whip by from the back of the Mercedes. The dusky green forest was a blur. The endless dome of equatorial sky seemed to hover just above them and yet looked impossibly far away. The sky down there was so different from the sky in Ocean City. The sunlight seemed sharper—not just stronger, but brighter, as though it could cut right into you and read your thoughts.

They passed small children carrying even smaller children on their backs. Women filed by with pyramids—of bananas, water cisterns, sacks of grain—balanced amazingly on their heads.

"How do they do that?" Kate whispered.

"They're trained from birth," Justin quipped. "I've seen them carry whole cars on their heads."

Kate slapped Justin's knee. "Don't be smart. Be respectful. That's probably hard."

"And it probably hurts," Justin said.

Kate leaned back and ran her hands over the plush velour seats. She watched the back of the chauffeur's head. How did they get there? When she and Justin had walked out of the boatyard and flagged a cab to the mysterious Trevor Chernak's house to find out more about the repair of the *Kate*, the new white Mercedes had pulled up in front of them. A young guy had waved them over and introduced himself as Jeremy, Mr. Chernak's chauffeur, as he opened the back door. At first Justin and Kate had just stood there, staring into the back of the car as if into a dangerous cave. Then Jeremy had cleared his throat, Justin had shrugged, and in they went.

"Why do you think he sent this car for us, anyway?" Kate asked.

"Why do you think he fixed my boat?" Justin replied. "If we find the answer to that question, I bet we'll find the answer to the other."

"I feel like I'm in a movie," she said. "Like some mysterious secret agent being whisked off on a secret mission."

"Hmmm. I like the sound of that, Miss Secret Agent."

Her hand traveled over his muscular chest,

his flat stomach. "That's *Ms.* Secret Agent to you," she said, smiling mischievously.

They felt the car lurch beneath them and sat up. They'd turned off the road and were headed for what looked like a wall of hedge. Then, amazingly, the hedge opened and led them down a shady road. On either side was the thick jungle. Birds were calling. The wind was rustling. It was like a different world, filled with a symphony of exotic sound.

"Whoa, would you look at that?" Justin whistled. A clearing opened in front of them to reveal a circular gravel driveway and a thatched-roof house that spread out of view and into the jungle itself. A sprawling turquoise swimming pool shimmered in the fading sunlight. A pair of topless local women relaxed in chaise lounges, flanked by tall empty glasses with miniumbrellas.

Kate noticed Justin's eyes following the women as the car pulled up to the door.

"Don't get whiplash, now," she murmured.

A young boy in baggy shorts ran to open their door.

"Mr. Chernak is waiting for you in the greenhouse," the boy said in his thick island accent.

"Of course," Kate said, walking confidently through the front door.

"Kate, wait up," Justin called after her.

"Come along, Justin," she said haughtily.

Then she winked. "This is fun," she whispered.

"This is weird," Justin grunted.

There were servants all over the place, but no one to tell them where to go. Doorways were everywhere. The house seemed to sprawl on forever.

"Welcome," bellowed a voice behind them.

Kate and Justin whirled around. A man in an all-white safari suit stood in a doorway with outstretched arms. He was a strange sight in his white uniform and white shoes, holding what looked like a riding crop. His brown hair was slicked back from his boyishly handsome face. How old was he? Kate couldn't tell. From second to second he looked anywhere from twenty to forty.

Justin didn't make a move. His face seemed to be frozen with distaste.

"Hello," Kate said.

"Allow me to introduce myself. I am Trevor—"

"What did you do to my boat?" Justin interrupted.

Kate threw Justin an annoyed look. They'd discussed how to handle the situation. They'd both agreed that it was weird for a complete stranger to spend a lot of money fixing a boat that wasn't his. But they also agreed that they'd give the guy a chance to explain. She could see, though, that Justin's patience was worn down.

"Trevor Chernak," the man finished, then smiled politely. "And you must be Kate Quinn. And Justin Garrett."

Kate couldn't figure out Chernak's accent. It was all over the place. It seemed caught between British and Brooklynese.

"Mr. Chernak, it was nice of you to send your car and have us out here and all," Justin said, "but you know why we're here, and to tell you the truth, I'd be a lot happier if you'd just tell us why you took it upon yourself to fix my boat."

Chernak smiled down at them like a benevolent father. "I'd be happy to, Mr. Garrett. Or may I call you Justin?"

"Justin's fine."

"Good, Justin. And . . . Kate? May I call you that?"

"Of course," Kate replied.

"Very good. Very good. This way, then, please," Chernak said with an affected British emphasis, and led them out toward the pool. "Let's have some refreshments while we get to know each other."

Outside, Chernak clapped his hands, and the two topless women jumped up and ran off into the house. He guided Kate and Justin toward a table, pulling out Kate's chair and helping her in.

"Thank you," Kate said uncomfortably. She had to admit it—this was getting a little strange.

"So do you like my new house?" Chernak said.

"It's okay," Justin said.

"It's beautiful," Kate said. "I've never seen so many species of flora in my life."

Chernak turned to Kate and looked at her with great interest. "So you are a horticulturist too?"

"I wouldn't say a—" Kate said, reddening.

"How wonderful," Chernak said. "I *adore* plants. I prefer them to people. I sensed right away that you liked them, too, Miss Quinn. I mean Kate. I just knew we'd get along."

Something about the way he said that made Kate shiver. She couldn't put her finger on it, but there was something about him that was creepy.

The women returned with a tray of iced tea and sandwiches. While they were setting the table, Chernak turned to Justin. He brought his fingers together as if he were praying and peered over them, looking long and hard into Justin's face. Then he nodded, as if he'd figured something out.

"I remember what it was like to be a poor sailor," Chernak said.

Justin glanced back at the outrageous, sprawling house. "You do?" he said, surprised.

"But of course. You think I got all this overnight? No, I started off with a little sailboat just like the *Kate*. I sailed around these islands by myself for years. I never had a home. My boat

56

was my home. I worked at whatever I could, making money just to get from port to port. Then"—he looked into the sky, as though searching the cloud patterns for the right phrase—"then I got lucky."

Chernak smiled meaningfully, but Kate knew he wouldn't tell them how.

"When I read about you in the newspaper," Chernak said, directing himself to Justin, "it made me think of myself at your age."

"Read about me?" Justin asked, sitting up.

"Very inspirational. A story for the ages. That tragedy a few months ago, when you were washed overboard and everyone thought you were dead."

Chernak smiled broadly. "And you were, Justin," he went on. "For two months, as far as the rest of the world was concerned, you were dead. People went on with their lives. But now look at you. A miracle. Brought back to life, sitting at my table." Chernak raised his glass. "To reincarnation," he toasted.

Justin and Kate peered at him suspiciously as they drank. But Kate had to admit it was the most delicious iced tea she'd ever had.

"So," Chernak said.

"So," Justin said. "The boat."

"Yes, of course, the boat. Well, you see, it seemed the natural thing to do."

"The natural thing to do?" Justin queried him. "To fix a stranger's boat without asking?"

"Come, come, Justin. After I read your story, I didn't know *who* would come and retrieve the boat, but I figured someone would. But for who you were, and who you might have been, and who I once was, I thought it was the least I could do in your honor. I think of it as the payback for my own good fortune in the name of your misfortune. That is, your *near* misfortune." Chernak grinned. "And, of course, we're *all* more fortunate that you're alive. Aren't we, Kate?"

"Yes, we are," Kate agreed.

She and Justin made eye contact. Justin seemed confused too, as if he wanted to be angry but just couldn't let himself be. Chernak had done them a great favor. He'd probably spent thousands fixing the boat.

"So, Justin, tell me," Chernak said, settling back in his seat. "Now that you have your boat back, do you have any special plans? A long, extended trip, perhaps?"

"As a matter of fact," Justin replied, "Kate and I are leaving the island."

"Where to, may I ask?" Chernak prodded him pleasantly.

"Just back to home base. Ocean City. You may have heard of it. A resort town on the northeast coast."

"Ocean City, Ocean City," Chernak repeated, tapping his fingers together. "Yes, I do recall. I am sure I sailed through there myself at some point. When I was your age. So, tell me, when do you shove off?"

Justin shifted uneasily in his seat. "Three days," he said.

"Three days, three days," Chernak echoed him distractedly, as if he were thinking of something else. "And when exactly do you plan on arriving in Ocean City? Any pit stops between here and there? A little sight-seeing in Florida, perhaps? The Keys? I hear the Keys are just lovely this time of year."

"Well," Justin said, "as a former sailor yourself, you probably remember that plans on the sea are meant to be broken."

"Of course, of course," Chernak said, smiling broadly. "But surely you must have in mind a ballpark figure. Four days? A week? A month?"

"To be honest, Mr. Chernak—"

Chernak held up his hand. "Trevor. Please."

"To be honest, Trevor," Justin said, "Kate and I were planning on a straight course. I have to get back and get a job. And Kate's going back to school soon. Besides, I didn't want to push the boat. After all, the last time—"

"The last time," Chernak said, nodding. "Of course. It's only natural that you'd want to get back to Ocean City as quickly as you can. After all, why push your luck?"

Something about Chernak's tone made Kate wince. He sounded as if he were issuing some sort of threat, or warning. He seemed just a little too pushy, a little too interested in them and their plans. All of it—this house, the iced tea, the favor he'd done them—seemed too good to be true. What exactly was going on?

FIVE

Connor stands at the lectern in his black turtle-neck and black linen blazer, reading the opening chapter of his newly published novel, Beach Blanket Begorra. *The auditorium is filled with editors and publishers and fans. His voice is calm and clear. He is in complete control. He can see that the old ladies in the first row have instantly fallen in love with his Irish accent, and he turns up the lilt just for them. The spotlights in his eyes, the quiet of the dark beyond them . . . he can feel his audience captured, enraptured. He has the New York literary world in the palm of his hand. He reads on. He hears knowing chuckles. He turns the pages, one, two, three. He turns to begin page four . . . but there isn't any page four! There is nothing but the back of the folder he carried his manuscript in. Where's page four? Where's page four? . . .*

Connor sat at his desk in a cold sweat, staring into the trash can at the multiple crumpled remains of page four. The nightmare had woken him at five in the morning and drawn him to his desk. But as the hour hand passed six, then seven, and as he heard Chelsea rise from bed and fumble around in the bathroom, getting ready to start her day, the nightmare was becoming more and more a reality. He picked up the editor's letter and reread it for the two-hundredth time: Yes, a major New York publishing house wanted to buy his novel. Yes, they were possibly willing to sign him to a multibook deal. Yes, they thought he was a prodigious talent.

"Blah, blah, blah," Connor said, tossing the letter aside. "I'm a legend in my own mind. I haven't even finished a single book! *And*, once again, I find myself unemployed. Fancy that."

Connor stared at the blank paper, then crumpled it and tossed it over his shoulder.

"Hey, there," Chelsea cried as the paper hit her square in the forehead.

Her caramel hands appeared before him, slowly massaging his shoulders and neck.

"How's it going, Mr. Literary Giant?" she asked.

"Mr. Literary Giant is quickly on the way to making himself into a giant literary fool."

"Come on, Connor," she said soothingly. "You've got to have at least as much confidence in yourself as they seem to have. I mean, listen to that letter."

Chelsea lifted the letter and began to pick out the juicy bits: "'Talent of enormous promise . . . lyrical, poetic . . .' and on and on. Connor, these people do this for a living. They wouldn't say it if they didn't mean it."

"Those people are vultures," Connor said. "They'd say anything to get what they want."

"But what they want is *you*," she said cheerfully. "They can't be wrong."

Connor yanked at his hair. "Maybe they're not wrong about those three chapters I sent them. But three chapters and an outline isn't a fully developed novel."

"Well, worrying isn't exactly going to get this novel done, either," Chelsea said, her voice firming with slight annoyance. "You've got to keep things in perspective. I mean, Connor, you're only twenty! You have at least seventy more years to finish this book and write a dozen or so more."

"Twenty? *Twenty?*" Connor cried, kneading his flame-red hair until it stood straight up as if his head were on fire. "Do you realize that Keats had written most of his great love poems by the time he was twenty? And that Carson McCullers finished *The Heart Is a Lonely Hunter* by the time she was *twenty-one*? And that by the time James Joyce was twenty-one, he'd written most of the stories in *Dubliners*, including 'The Dead,' which is only the bloody greatest story in the English language? So you think it's a comfort to be twenty and to have written only three bloody chapters of bloody *Beach Bloody Blanket Bloody Begorra*? Twenty's over the hill! Twenty's practically retired! Twenty could well be literary failure!"

"Connor, if only you calmed . . . I mean stopped complain—" Chelsea caught herself. "I don't think you're being fair to yourself, Connor. You can't compare yourself to them. It's ri—"

Chelsea saw his lips pout with hurt feelings. "I mean, of course, you're just as good as they were. Just as talented. Just as—"

Connor rolled his eyes. She just couldn't say anything right. She threw up her hands. "I'd just do my best if I were you," she said quickly.

"Easy for you to say," Connor snapped. "You don't have an anxious editor breathing down your neck."

"Well," Chelsea said, looking around the room, "I don't see anybody in this room but you and me. And, by the way, my offer to write a few lines for you still stands."

"You!" Connor shrieked in horror. "I love you,

Chels, but this isn't about you. There's no place for you in this book."

"No place for me, huh?"

"That's right. It's all me, sink or swim. The artist's life is a lonely life."

"The *artist's* life! What about *married* life?" Chelsea narrowed her eyes. "I thought marriage was about throwing each other the occasional lifeline when we needed it. Connor, we're supposed to help each other out."

Connor threw Chelsea one of his get-with-the-program looks. "Come on, Chels. This is real life. Believe me, I wish you could help me. But wishes and dreams aren't going to get this book done. This is what I've been waiting for my whole life. And I'm choking. I'm a fake, a fraud."

Chelsea looked down at Connor as if she didn't know whether to kiss him or shoot him and put him out of his misery.

"Connor," she said, "maybe coming down to Washington to see my cousin's baby will do you some good. You know, clear your head. Maybe being a godparent will give you confidence or something. . . ."

"Washington! You still expect me to go to Washington? Don't you understand? Don't you *want* me to succeed? This is my life. This is the moment I've been waiting for. I can't think about babies! I can't think about marriage. This is for real now. I have to think about this," he said, gesturing to the stack of blank paper. "Until it's done: this, this, and only this."

Chelsea propped her hands on her hips. "This, this, and only this? Fine! I'm going on my own," she said, and stomped out of the room.

"Grace? . . . Grace? . . . If you're not going to eat anything, don't you think you should close the door?"

Grace's head snapped up, and she turned to find her roommate Marta surveying her from her wheelchair in the kitchen doorway.

"Sorry, what did you say?" Grace asked.

"How *long* have you been staring into that refrigerator?"

"Just a minute or two. Why?"

"Grace," Marta pointed out, shaking her head, "you have goose bumps, and your skin is turning blue."

Grace looked down at herself. Then she took another look into the refrigerator, sighed, and shut the door.

"It's a very common affliction," Marta said, rolling into the kitchen. "When there's nothing appetizing to eat, it's easy to linger around and wait, as though eventually something will show up on one of those shelves that will make us happy."

"Hmmm."

"But me," Marta continued breezily, "I'm easy to please." She opened the refrigerator door, reached in, and pulled out an apple.

"Keeps the doctor away," she said happily as she bit into it. "It's also great breakfast food. Cleans out your system. And it's best to eat fruit by itself, so that you get all the vitamins and nutrients—"

"Marta?" Grace interrupted. "In case you've forgotten, I'm usually in a rotten mood in the morning. Today is no exception."

"Sorry." Marta blushed and pushed her dark hair off her face. "I'm a little wound up, I guess."

Grace fell into a chair by the little breakfast table and dropped her head into her hands.

"Okay," she sighed. "Lay it on me."

"What?" Marta asked, a little too innocently.

"Whatever it is you're about to tell me," Grace answered. "You're hyper, chipper, nervous, and talkative. And I'm already in a crappy mood—don't take it personally—so don't worry, you probably can't make it any worse."

"I'm sorry, Grace," Marta said, her fingers tapping the wheels of her chair. "I hope this isn't a bad time . . . but I wanted to tell you . . . um . . . that I'm moving out. Not because I don't love it here, of course," Marta rushed on, "and I know you've done so much for me already,

67

putting in the elevator, and the rails in my bathroom downstairs, and I feel somehow guilty about all of that—since it's not likely that you'll have another roommate in a wheelchair—but Dominic and I . . . well, we just want to . . . on a trial basis, of course, because it would never be the same if we tried it here—"

"You're moving in with Dominic."

"Yes." Marta nodded.

Grace sighed. Why wasn't she surprised? she wondered. Kate and Justin were gone. David was leaving her. And now Marta. *Everyone is gone or going,* Grace thought. *Except me. I've got a house here now. With another room that's about to be empty.*

"So," Grace said, forcing herself to smile. It wasn't fair to make Marta feel bad, when she was so obviously happy. "You and Dominic are going to play house, huh?"

Marta blushed. "Look, I'm not ready to get married," she said. "But I do love him. And I'm at least ready to take the next step from where we are now. I want to be with him, and I don't want to have to worry about Roan sleeping next door, if you know what I mean."

"Oh, yeah, I know what you mean. You're a good young woman, Marta," Grace said mockingly. "It wouldn't be right for you to corrupt a little girl."

"And not just any little girl." Marta smiled.

"That's right!" Grace cried, grinning, and shaking her fist. "That's my little girl! Whoa! Hold on! Speaking of little girls," Grace said suddenly, "what about your father? How's he going to take to all this?"

"Oh, you mean Luis Salgado, Head Lifeguard and Notorious Striker of Fear into the Hearts of Young Men Interested in His Daughter?" Marta asked.

"That's the one," Grace said.

Marta cackled and then shook her head. "Well, to be perfectly honest, I don't know."

"Don't tell me," Grace warned.

"I haven't told him," Marta admitted. "But he likes Dominic. He respects him. Dominic's from our old neighborhood. And he's Hispanic. Not that my father was ever racist, but he's pretty excited by the fact that Dominic is the first non-Anglo guy I've ever been interested in. And Dad can relate to him. It does matter sometimes to have that cultural-identity thing. It helps you understand a person better," Marta said seriously.

"And also helps you forgive them sometimes," Grace said softly, thinking of all Marta had told her about Dominic's past.

Strange as it seemed—almost impossible, really—Dominic had been a member of a notorious street gang back in L.A. And eight years

69

ago Marta had been caught in the cross fire of a gang shoot-out. The bullet that had paralyzed her had been fired by Dominic. Dominic and Marta had fallen in love before she'd found out who he really was, and what he had done. Grace knew Marta had dealt with a lot, and put a lot behind her, in order to forgive Dominic and move on with her life, and with him.

"That's part of it," Marta agreed. "Although I doubt Dad will ever know *everything*. There are some things a father would never be able to forgive," she said meaningfully.

"You're probably right about that," Grace agreed.

"Anyway, Grace," Marta said, "Dominic and I are going out today to look for apartments. I wanted to tell you right away. And I wanted to thank you. For everything."

Grace shrugged. "What'd I do, anyway, besides slap some steel tubing on a few walls? And who says I won't use that elevator again?"

"If you can't find another paraplegic, at least you can sell rides on it to the neighborhood kids," Marta suggested.

Grace laughed. "Yep," she said, "I'm going to miss you."

"Well, you've got me for a little while yet," Marta said, pulling her van keys out of her purse and rolling herself out of the kitchen to the front door. "And do feel free to shower me with gifts and kindness during that time."

"Don't push your luck."

"See ya later," Marta called. The sound of the door closing reverberated through the empty house.

"Great," Grace muttered, shading her eyes against the sun as she walked onto the balcony and looked out over the ocean. "In addition to finding a new person to run my one empty beach stand, which most likely *won't* happen by this afternoon, which means I'll be getting up early tomorrow morning to do it *myself,* I need to find a new roommate, too. Unless I want to be utterly without company. Except for two sixteen-year-olds." She sighed.

"Not drinking is one thing," she continued. "But not drinking *and* hanging out with sixteen-year-olds is just a little too depressing."

Just then she heard laughter and the sound of a screen door opening. She looked down and saw Bo and Roan walking out of the house onto the patio below her. Roan pulled her white-blond hair into a ponytail while Bo slipped his sunglasses on. Then they reached for each other's hands and headed out onto the beach.

"Now, that's *really* depressing," Grace muttered, turning her back on the young lovers. "Maybe it's the not drinking I should reconsider."

71

Quickly she turned back to the ocean and looked frantically for Bo and Roan. She spotted them down the beach chasing each other in and out of the surf.

"Drinking is *not* the answer," she reminded herself angrily, her eyes hungrily feeding on the two people who she knew still needed her. Needed her to be responsible. Needed her to take care of them. To take care of herself.

Marta was getting out of her van when Grace drove up with a stormy expression on her face.

Marta waited for her at the front door.

"Grace? You okay?"

"Hmmm," was the response as Grace brushed by her, walking like a zombie.

Marta wheeled into the house just behind her. Grace wandered into the living room and plopped down onto one of the soft beige sofas.

"You must be upset," Marta suggested, rolling up beside her.

"Why do you say that?" Grace asked distractedly.

"Why? You're sitting in the living room," Marta pointed out, as though it were obvious. "No one ever sits in the living room unless someone's run away, been found with another woman, or been stabbed," Marta said, remembering the last three times she'd ever seen anyone actually hanging out in the living room.

"Hmmm," Grace muttered. "You've got a point."

"Well," Marta pressed. "Are you going to tell me?"

"How was house hunting?" Grace suddenly asked.

"Nice try. House hunting was exhausting. There's no place in O.C. as comfortable or as well set up as your house, Grace. It may take a few days to find something even half as good."

Grace grunted again.

"But we're still looking. So, now, what's up with you?"

Grace dropped her head back onto the couch and closed her eyes. "David's leaving," she said softly. "Going to Taiwan for at least a year to fly jets. We just had our last flight together."

"Well," Marta said, truly surprised. "I guess that accounts for the long face. I'm sorry."

"Yeah," Grace admitted. "Me too."

"But he's coming back?" Marta asked.

Grace shook her head.

"Ouch," Marta muttered, suddenly feeling terribly guilty. David was leaving the country and she was leaving the house. No wonder Grace looked depressed. She was being totally abandoned.

"Forget what I said," Marta spoke before she knew it. "I'm not moving out."

Grace cracked an eye and looked at her skeptically. "Please. Don't make me feel so desperate. Do you really think I would let you stay just to keep me company? Just because *my* love life is in the toilet doesn't mean that *yours* ought to be. I'm not that cruel, you know."

Marta chuckled.

"Well," Grace admitted, "I used to be that cruel. But I'm not anymore and that's what matters."

"Are you sure you don't want me to stay?"

"Of course I want you to stay," Grace cried, "but I won't let you. I'd hate to be quite so pathetic." She looked away.

"Well," Marta offered, "I could stay another month or two—"

Grace leaped up. "Get out! Get out while you can," she cried. "If you stay here with me, you'll be a cynic in seven days. Don't worry about me. I have Bo and Roan. They'll keep me company."

Marta laughed. "I'm glad that you still have a sense of humor."

"Yes, I'm taking up skateboarding, did I tell you? I'll have a whole new group of young friends before you can blink."

"What about a new roommate?" Marta asked.

"Well," Grace cocked her head and grinned. "If you really want to do something for me . . ."

"Okay," Marta agreed. "I guess it's the least I can do."

"That's right."

"So," Marta prompted, "what are you looking for?"

"What do you mean?" Grace asked.

"What kind of roommate should I advertise for?" Marta explained.

"Hmmm. You mean animal, vegetable, or mineral? How about human? Over eighteen? Preferably potty trained?"

Marta laughed. "No, I mean female or *male?*"

"It doesn't matter to me." Grace shrugged. "I'm off men—for at least a year or two."

Right, Marta said to herself, *and I'm running the Boston Marathon this year.* She nodded and smiled. "Whatever you say, Grace," she agreed amiably.

But now Marta had a plan. At least she knew what kind of roommate to look for. Grace needed some perking up, and Marta was determined to help.

Six

"You're like a mother hen," Kate said with a laugh, following Justin as he looked over his boat, checking carefully for any more mysterious "repairs." "You can't stand to see anyone else touching your baby. Boy, if you have daughters, you're going to be hell to live with."

Justin turned to look at her and cocked his eyebrow, the side of his mouth curling into a grin.

"I'll be hell to live with," Justin agreed. "But you'll learn to handle it."

"Who says I'll have to?" Kate shot back.

"It's just one of those well-known female patterns. First she starts thinking about kids. Then she picks out names for the kids. The next thing the poor guy knows, he's married, and the rest of his life is a battle to find a full-time job with good benefits."

"Ha. That shows how much you know, buster," Kate said. "You're the one who wants to hang out on a boat or beach for the rest of your life. You're just the type of guy to try to snare some young, ambitious woman and get her to support you to the end of your lazy days."

"Mmmm, sounds good," Justin said, wrapping one arm around her and pulling her close. "Are you applying?"

"Only on a short-term basis for now. Remember," Kate said, turning serious, "you have me for only a few months. I'm back in school come September."

"I know, I know." Justin sighed. "But we haven't even left yet. Just wait." His voice was low and sexy, a light glinting in his eyes that made Kate's heart beat faster. "We've got long weeks ahead of us." His hand traveled down her back, pulling her tightly against him. "Just you, me, the stars, and the sea."

"Right," Kate said, her eyes turning mischievous. "And you know what they say about a man and his boat."

"Hmm?" Justin sighed, nuzzling her ear.

"It's not the size of the boat," Kate whispered, holding back her laughter, "it's the motion of the ocean."

"Kate!" Justin cried.

"I'm just getting into the mood." She laughed.

"Besides, it won't be quite as romantic as you make it sound. It's not just 'you, me, the stars, and the sea,' you know."

"Who else?"

Kate pointed to the familiar shaggy shape sprawled across the bow.

"Our friend Mooch, remember?" Kate grinned. "The one who loves to sleep between us."

"Oh, him. He's just a bit protective."

"He's not protective," Kate amended. "He's jealous. And right now he needs to go for a walk. He's the laziest dog I ever saw. Learned that from you, too, I guess. Come on, rouse him and let's go," Kate prodded, pulling away from Justin and picking up her knapsack. "We've only got a few more days to explore, and I want to do some sight-seeing."

"Let's let him stay here and keep watch, huh?" Justin pleaded. "I hate to wake him from a deep sleep. He's all cranky then."

"Good idea. A cranky dog isn't my idea of a sight-seeing partner, either. It's not every day you find yourself in a tropical paradise."

"Paradise" was certainly the right word, Kate thought later, looking left and right down the beach. Her sandals dangled from one hand, her other hand held Justin's tightly. The white sand was warm and smooth beneath her bare feet. It was early evening, and the sun was just beginning to drop into the water, outlining the trees in a warm red glow.

"I thought spending summers in O.C. had taught me what it was like to live near the ocean," she said softly. "How can this place be so different?"

"It really is a different world," Justin agreed. "It's not O.C. Not by a long shot."

"I don't think I'd ever get anything done at all if I lived here."

Even in the main town, she thought, where most of the tourists were, the event of the day seemed to be sitting under an umbrella somewhere having a cold drink.

"Most of the work is done before you wake up," Justin said. "This is still a fishing community. The fishing boats are back in by nine or ten o'clock. Then the workers have the rest of the day to take cover from the sun."

"That's true," Kate admitted. "But, still, there's so much that could be done. . . ."

She was thinking of all the little villages they'd visited that day. Everywhere they'd gone, the men were crowded into small cafés, sitting around radios or tiny black-and-white televisions, listening to old rock-and-roll songs or watching reruns of *Dallas* and *Falcon Crest*.

Kate had wondered where the women were.

Then she and Justin had taken their rented bicycles down the dirt roads and found them—clustered around the thatch houses of the small villages, or gathered around the wells, chattering and watching flocks of children scramble in and out of the brush.

The local community was definitely divided. Men did one thing, and women did another. Everywhere she went, Kate couldn't help thinking of grassroots projects she'd want to start if she stayed. Awareness programs for health care, education . . .

"Always changing the world, aren't you, Kate?" Justin said, as if reading her mind. He squeezed her hand, perhaps in sympathy. "But remember, this is a different world from the one you know. Before you start trying to tell people how to have 'better' lives, you'd better make sure they're unhappy with the ones they've got."

"I know. But even though this place is beautiful, I still see things that make me want to do *something*. I can relax for a while. But there's a difference between taking a breather and not breathing at all."

"This is just one island, Kate, in an ocean full of places to go. And if you've seen something new here, just imagine how many other things you could learn in other places. See, I told you it would be worth traveling," Justin said.

"Hey, I already admitted you were right, and believe it or not, these few days have helped me see even more clearly what kinds of things I'd like to do with my life. I was afraid traveling with you would make me lose sight of important things," Kate said.

"Ahh, but if you hadn't come," Justin joked, "the only important thing you'd have lost sight of would've been me!"

Justin grabbed her around the waist and danced her up the beach to a small restaurant that sat just below the hanging palm trees. Colorful lanterns hung in the trees, and there were white lights strung along the beams and poles of the open patio.

"Time for a meal, I think," Justin sighed. "All this relaxing is making me hungry."

"It's hard work enjoying yourself so much," Kate agreed.

"But first," Justin said, grabbing her shoes away from her and throwing them under an empty table as music from a jukebox in the corner suddenly came on, "a dance with my island princess."

Kate blushed and looked down at her sarong. She'd felt a bit like a silly tourist when she'd run into one of the shops in town to get it, but now, seeing the look in Justin's eyes, she was happy she'd done it.

It was wrapped around her waist a few times and hugged her hips, a slightly sheer material dyed in a beautiful green-and-violet swirl. She knew it set off her tan and her sun-streaked blond hair. *This is one thing I'll have to hide from Chelsea when I get home,* Kate thought to herself, immediately remembering Chelsea's penchant for borrowing clothes, especially bright, sexy clothes like this.

She batted her eyes playfully and let Justin lead her around the makeshift dance floor, which was just a patch of beach beneath the canopy of the restaurant.

They ordered their food—grilled fish-and-vegetable specials—and leaned back in their chairs, staring at each other over the rims of their tropical-fruit drinks.

Justin winked and wiggled his eyebrows.

"Paradise," Kate agreed.

"If you think this is paradise," Justin said in a low voice, "just wait until later." He lifted her arm and planted a soft, warm kiss on the inside of her wrist. "I'll show you what not breathing feels like."

"I can hardly catch my breath now," Kate said, leaning over to give him a deep kiss.

When they broke apart, Kate spied their waiter making his way over with an enormous tray piled high with food. "Oh, good, here comes dinner. Suddenly I'm very hungry."

"Eat up," Justin said. "You'll need to keep up your strength."

But just as the waiter was about to reach them, a red-haired girl came scurrying from the bathroom, tripped trying to navigate between the tables, and stumbled into the waiter. Kate watched sadly as the tray sailed through the air and landed with a soft thud in the sand, followed closely by the waiter and the girl.

"Oh, my God, I'm so sorry," the girl spluttered as she tried to untangle herself, her face flaming as red as her hair. She leaned over to help the waiter, who was reaching for the tray, and bumped his elbow, sending the bowl he'd just picked up out of his fingers and farther away into the sand.

"Sorry!" she cried, reaching for the bowl. "I'm terribly sorry, please, let me help you—"

"No!" the waiter cried, all but pushing her away. He smiled shakily. "Really, mademoiselle, please. You just sit, please. No help. Thank you, please."

The girl was finally standing, and she turned to face Kate and Justin. Her bright-red hair was pulled into a lopsided ponytail high on her head. And her thick black glasses sat unevenly on her face. Thin, impossibly pale arms poked out of an oversize white T-shirt. And a pair of long flowered shorts fell almost to her knees. She was blushing furiously.

"I'm so sorry," she said, looking at the ground. "About your food. I just . . ." She sighed and shrugged her shoulders and looked away. Kate thought she was blinking back tears.

"I'm just so *clumsy* sometimes," the girl went on. "I'm really sorry."

"That's all right," Kate said quickly.

"It's not as though we were *starving* or anything," Justin added.

Kate shot him a dirty look.

"Really?" the girl said sadly. "I'd like to . . . do something for you. I feel so bad. Can I . . . treat you to your meal?"

"Of course not," Kate said. "It was an accident. It could happen to anybody." The girl was visibly relieved. *She must not have much money,* Kate thought, feeling sorry for her.

"But things like this seem to happen to me so much more *often* than to other people," the girl said, sounding forlorn.

"Why don't you join us for dinner?" Kate suddenly suggested, ignoring the poke Justin gave her under the table. "That is, if you're not meeting someone else?"

"Oh, no," the girl said quickly. "No one else."

"Then, please, sit down." Kate smiled at her.

"Really?" The girl looked quickly at Justin. "I

mean . . . I don't want to interrupt anything. You're not . . . you're not on your honeymoon or anything, are you?" she suddenly asked, taking a step away. "Because I'd hate to intrude—"

"No, no," Justin cut her off. "Really. You're not intruding." He kicked Kate under the table. "Please join us."

"I'm Kate, and this is Justin," Kate offered.

"Oh, sorry." The girl blushed again. "Allegra. That's my name." She pulled over a chair and unfolded it, catching her T-shirt on the back of it as she sat. She was about to topple over when Justin reached out and grabbed the chair. Allegra yanked at her shirt, ripping it free, and sat quickly, before anything else could befall her.

"My mother thought it was a graceful name," Allegra said, "though I seem to have turned out anything but."

"Are you here with your parents?" Kate asked.

"Oh, no," Allegra said, looking away. "I don't live at home anymore. I . . . uh, I came with a . . . friend."

"A friend?" Justin asked.

"Yes." Allegra hesitated. "A man, actually."

"He's not joining you for dinner?" Kate asked. "Is he out sight-seeing, or on business or something?"

"Oh, I'm not sure what he's doing right now," Allegra said slowly. "If he's having his way, he's

85

probably doing some kind of sight-seeing, but not the kind you'd write home about, if you know what I mean."

"Are you saying you're on your own here?" Kate asked.

"Well, since this morning, yes," Allegra admitted. "I thought he was just a nice man. I met him in Florida. I was working in a little shop there. And he was really nice, and . . . older. Like an older brother or an uncle, you know?"

Justin glanced over at Kate and rolled his eyes. He was mouthing something to her, but she couldn't make it out. So he leaned over, put his arm around her, covered his mouth with his other hand, and coughed in her ear. "Naive!" he coughed. "Naive!"

Kate smiled stiffly and pushed him away.

"Anyway," Allegra continued, "he said he was coming down here, and he asked me if I wanted to come, too. And of course I thought it would be really nice. He was fine, too, for the whole trip. Until last night." She stopped.

"Did he—?" Kate couldn't bring herself to ask.

"Well," Allegra said, glancing at Justin and blushing again. "He wanted to. I mean, we had a nice dinner, and he drank an awful lot . . . and then he tried . . . but *you* know—I just left."

"You left?" Kate asked. "Where did you go?"

"I just got my stuff and left," Allegra said. "I slept on the beach last night. And that was it."

"Wow," Justin said. "That's too bad. I'm really sorry."

"Sorry if I'm being nosy," Kate said, "but can I ask how old you are?"

"Sure. People ask me that all the time. I'm nineteen, but last night at dinner they thought I was his daughter. His daughter, can you believe it? They thought I was twelve or something." Allegra shook her head.

I can believe it, Kate thought, surprised to know Allegra was the same age as she and Justin.

"I've been on my own for a while," Allegra offered. "Here and there. But mostly on the coasts, near the ocean. I love the water," she said happily. "In fact, sleeping on the beach is one of my favorite things, so I didn't mind last night too much at all."

"I agree." Justin smiled. "Sleeping on the beach can be wonderful." He squeezed Kate's leg, reminding her of the nights they'd spent on the beach together. "Almost as good as sleeping on the water," he went on. "You'll see what I mean," he said to Kate. "Sleeping on a sailboat out at sea is about a thousand times better than a measly waterbed."

"Oh, I love to sail," Allegra cried, her eyes shining. "It's the only time, really, when I'm not worried about falling over or breaking something. I guess I have better sea legs than land legs."

"Well, I sure don't have *my* sea legs yet," Kate admitted. "It may take me a while to get used to the motion."

"You still have time to get used to it," Justin reminded her.

"Are you going on a long trip?" Allegra asked excitedly.

Justin nodded. "At least a few weeks."

"Wow. How excellent. Where are you sailing?" Allegra asked. "That is . . . if you don't mind my asking."

"Not at all." Kate laughed.

"We're sailing my boat back home. To Ocean City. It's in the States. East Coast."

"You're kidding." Allegra gasped.

"You know Ocean City?" Kate asked.

"Know it? This is so odd. I mean . . . that's where I'm trying to go."

"Do you live there?" Justin asked.

"Well, no," Allegra said. "I mean, I never have before, but my aunt and uncle just moved there, and I thought I might be able to stay with them for a bit. Isn't that weird?" she asked. "Small world. . . . Their name is Wolfe," she said excitedly. "Do you know them?"

"Sorry." Justin shook his head. "Never met them."

"Well, they're young, but not as young as us. They don't really hang out on the beach. Wow," she went on, "it's so nice we met. I can't believe it. When I get back, if I make it to Ocean City, maybe we can hang out. Now that I'll know somebody there, it's not so frightening to think of moving to a new place." Allegra's eyes were wistful, and the corners of her mouth twitched a little as she tried to smile.

Kate wanted to reach out and squeeze her hand. *How many times has she moved?* she wondered. *How many new cities has she been where she didn't know anyone?*

"How are you going to get home?" Kate asked.

"Oh, I'm sorry." Allegra blushed. "Please, I hope you don't think . . . I mean I just couldn't believe the coincidence. I'm not asking . . . I mean, don't feel you have to . . ."

"Allegra," Kate interrupted. "Do you have a way to get home?"

"Not yet," Allegra admitted softly. "But, please, don't worry about me." She forced a smile. "I'll find a way. I always do."

SEVEN

"Ooh yes, ooh yes," Chelsea heard Connor yelp from the next room. "Brilliant. Absolutely, unequivocally brilliant."

He appeared in the doorway, his clothes in a shambles, his reddish-brown hair looking like an overgrown patch of weed, and his pupils the size of quarters from drinking gallons of black coffee.

"Ooh yes," Connor said, and danced a little jig.

"Uh, happy, Connor?" Chelsea asked.

"You, lassie, are married to a genius of the highest ordinance," Connor said.

"Please, go on," Chelsea said.

"I am unlocking levels of understanding of the human condition that precious few even possess the key to."

Chelsea feigned total absorption in every

word Connor uttered. "Connor, you're amazing. Yesterday you were climbing the walls, saying over and over what a worthless prig you are."

Connor winced. "I actually said 'prig'?"

"And that you had no business laying your fingers on a typewriter ever again."

"Really? I said that?"

"In fact, last night you came in here begging me to take your typewriter to the boardwalk and throw it into the ocean," Chelsea said.

Connor scratched his head. "Wow."

"And yesterday afternoon you said you'd give me anything—including your firstborn, which I already have rights to, by the way—to build a bonfire and incinerate your typewriter until it was just a mound of charred metal and melted plastic."

"I must have been desperate," Connor said. His face contorted with confusion, then elation. "Well, last night was last night. And tonight is tonight. Shall I read to you, Chels? Shall I read?"

"Please do," Chelsea said, putting aside the magazine she was perusing.

Connor lifted the page, extended his arm, and opened his mouth. Then he shut it. "I can't do it," he said. "I just can't. I can't show this to anyone, not until I'm done."

"You know something, Connor?"

"What?"

"You're crazy."

"I agree," Connor replied quickly, suddenly looking downcast. "But most great writers are crazy."

"I take it back. You're not crazy. You're lunatic."

"Thank you, my sweet. I take that as a high compliment." He spun on his heels. "Well, back to the salt mines."

"Honestly, Connor, won't you let me look at any of it? Maybe I can help," Chelsea called out to him as he headed back into the next room. Connor stopped and turned around. "I've been known to offer good criticism every now and then," she said.

"Criticism!" Connor cried. "I don't need criticism. I need inspiration!"

"Oh," Chelsea said, sagging a little deeper into the couch. "God forbid I should ever offer you *inspiration*."

Come on, Chels, she told herself. *You know he's under a lot of pressure. Just go with it until he gets through this.*

"Okay, Connor," she said cheerily. "So what can I do?"

Suddenly Connor's face twisted with pain. "Well, there *is* the matter of a little knot in the back of my neck from my feverish forays at the typewriter."

Chelsea smiled and extended her arms to

Connor. "Where are those big bad feverish forays hurting you?"

Connor knelt in front of Chelsea. "Here," he said, bowing his head and pointing to the back of his neck.

As Chelsea rubbed, Connor moaned with pleasure. "And here," he said, pointing to his right shoulder.

"Uh-huh."

"And here," he said, pointing to his left.

It felt to Chelsea like years since she'd gotten this close to Connor. She'd almost forgotten how attractive she found him. Her fingers traveled down his back. Her touch became softer, less athletic and more affectionate. Eventually she took his face in her hands and brought it up to hers. She leaned down to kiss him. And when her lips touched his, his eyes popped open, and he leaped to his feet. It was exactly the opposite reaction Chelsea had expected. She sat back with surprise.

"Come on, Chels. What're you doing?"

"What am I doing?" Chelsea asked. "I'm your wife. You're my husband."

"Yeah? So?"

"So I was, you know—" Chelsea said, her face darkening.

"I can't spare any time for *this*," Connor said distastefully. "I'm a man on a mission."

"You may be on a mission," Chelsea murmured, "but the way it's been around here lately, I wouldn't know if you're still a man."

"What was that?"

"Nothing," Chelsea said irritably. "Forget it. It's not like I'm trying to keep you from your own greatness. It's just that you've been looking right through me lately, like I'm not even here. I want to help you, but I'm beginning to feel invisible. Do you even know that I'm here, Connor?"

Connor smiled as he would at a child.

"Of course I know you're here, Chelsea," he said. "But I've got work to do. Don't you want me to be successful?"

Chelsea opened her mouth, but there was too much she wanted to say, and it wouldn't all come out. Connor bent down and barely brushed her cheek with his lips, then scampered off into the next room, slamming the door behind him.

Don't I want him to be successful? Chelsea repeated to herself, glaring angrily at the closed door. *Have I ever wanted him to be anything but successful?*

Marta had spent the entire day interviewing so many unsuitable roommates that she was beginning to feel faint. So when she looked up and saw him standing in front of her, she thought she might be hallucinating.

At first all she could see were his eyes. They were the deepest, bluest eyes she'd ever seen. *The sky doesn't even come in that color,* she thought briefly. There were small flecks of gold floating in the incredible blue that seemed to pierce her right to the heart. And his voice—it was deep, lulling, and sensual, music like none she'd ever heard before.

"Excuse me," the voice repeated, "but I asked if the room was still available."

"Oh, uh, s-sorry," she stammered. "Did you ask about the room?"

"Is it still available?" he said again.

Marta couldn't take her eyes off him. His face was tan and chiseled. He had cheekbones that should have been illegal and a long, firm nose. Sensuous lips. Gorgeous sandy-blond hair that swept back from his face. Marta dropped her gaze and realized it got even better.

"You work for the Beach Patrol?" Marta exclaimed, noticing the distinctive, and impossibly sexy, red shorts. Like every good lifeguard, this one wore his shorts on, and off, the beach—and nothing else.

"I just started today. Boy, the guy who heads it is really tough."

"Hmmm," Marta agreed.

"You know him? Luis Salgado? Back home we'd call him a burr on an ass."

"That sounds about right," Marta said with a smile. "I know him. He's my father."

Instantly the remarkable face turned a shade of beautifully deep crimson.

"I'm sorry," he said. "I didn't mean to insult you."

"That's okay," she said softly. "Anytime."

"Does he live here?" he asked, suddenly agitated.

"Oh, no," Marta cried. "This is my friend's house. I'm just looking for a new place."

"You don't like it here?"

"Oh, I love it!" Marta said quickly. "I'm just moving in with my boyfriend."

"Oh." There it was again. The Incredible Blush. The Incredible Hunk with an Incredible Blush.

"Well, you know," he continued, "you never did tell me whether the room was still available."

"Oh, right." Marta studied him again. This was beyond her wildest imagination. She'd had no idea people really came this way. It was almost awe inspiring, Marta realized. He was a work of art. Truly perfect.

And truly perfect for Grace.

"I couldn't have done better if I'd made you up," Marta said, without thinking.

"Excuse me?"

"Sorry." She chuckled. "What I meant to say is that the room is officially taken."

"Oh. That's too bad," he said. "This is a really nice place."

"What I meant," Marta explained, "is that it's taken by you."

"Really?" he asked. "You mean it?"

"Sure," Marta said. "So now that you're moving in, what's your name?"

"Carr Savett," he said, breaking into a big grin as he looked around.

Grace is going to love me for this.

Grace looked up as she suddenly found herself sitting in shadow. It was like an eclipse of the sun. Before her stood a large man sprouting balls of muscle. He flashed a row of gleaming white teeth.

"May I help you?" Grace said from behind her beach stand. She put aside her novel, Edith Wharton's *The Age of Innocence*, and stood.

"Uh, you sure can," the gleaming mouth said, turning around to smirk at a group of similarly pruned muscle-heads.

Grace crossed her arms over her chest and rolled her eyes. It was her bad luck that she hadn't changed her bikini selection since her Days of Men and Wine. Now that David was gone, she would have to buy a new suit or two if she didn't want to keep attracting the attention of boneheads in possession of not a voltage worth of brainpower. All day long guys had pretended to peruse her selection of magazines and suntan oils and assorted beach paraphernalia while actually peering down her cleavage.

"How much is this SPF fifteen?" the guy said.

"Six ninety-nine," Grace answered.

"How much is this SPF twenty?"

"Six ninety-nine. You know, the price is right there on the bottle. It's that little square of paper with the numbers on it."

"Oh, uh-huh. *The Age of Innocence*," the guy said, picking up Grace's novel. "That a romance or something?"

Grace snatched the book out of his hands. "Not for sale," she snapped.

"What about you? You for sale? Or better yet, for rent?"

The guy started laughing, and Grace smiled and laughed along, reaching for her large cup of iced coffee and oh so accidentally giving it a little shove, sending it over the edge of the table and down the front of the guy's bikini shorts.

"Oops," Grace said as the guy leaped away and grabbed at his shorts. "I'm so sorry. Here," she said, flipping him a quarter. "That's for the dry-cleaning bill. Now get lost."

The guy was so stunned he didn't even respond. He simply turned and waddled quickly toward the changing rooms down the beach.

Grace moaned as she collapsed into her chair.

When would her life get off this roller-coaster ride? One day she was standing on top of the world with a man she thought she could love, and the next she was standing on a beach of hot, hot sand, totally alone, fending off every creep on the East Coast.

She looked left down the beach at the stand she'd put Roan in charge of. Men were flocking around her like gulls around a picnic blanket. Except Roan was tipping her head back in laughter, smiling away.

"Hey, there, good-looking," came another oily male voice.

"Hey, there yourself," Grace snapped. "The prices are all clearly marked. I don't have anything that's not on the display. No, I don't know when high tide is. And no, I don't have a phone number because I don't have a phone, because I don't like to be bothered or talked to or asked out or proposed to. Understand?" Grace cried after the retreating figure.

She reached down and threw her T-shirt over her bikini top, hoping that would diminish her appeal.

Just as she had herself comfortable again in her chair and had gotten back into her novel, there was another interruption.

"How do you like it?" said a voice.

Grace squinted up into the sun. She couldn't

see a thing, but she could tell it was another guy.

"That's disgusting!" Grace said. "Get lost!"

"Well, why are you reading it if you think it's disgusting?"

"What?" Grace asked. "What are you talking about?"

"The book," the guy said. "I asked you how you liked it."

"Oh."

The guy walked out of the sun and stood where Grace could see him. He wasn't tall; his biceps weren't bigger than his thighs. He wore little wire-rim glasses that made him look like a librarian from the nineteenth century. And his bathing suit—puke green trunks, not particularly eye-catching. He was no one she would notice. Just another nerd trying to hit on her, not knowing how.

"The SPF fifteen is six ninety-nine," Grace grunted.

"Excuse me?"

"I said, the SPF—" Grace realized he wasn't really interested. She just shrugged and put her nose back in her book.

She read a few more lines but the guy hadn't moved. She looked up and sighed.

"High tide's at eight twenty-five tonight," she said.

"Really," the guy said. "That's nice." He

kicked at the sand. "What did you think of the big dinner scene?"

"Big what?" Grace said, sitting up. "What are you talking about?"

"Your novel," he said, motioning to the book in Grace's hands. "Around page two hundred, depending on the edition, of course."

Grace peered down at the page. "Not there yet," she said, then looked up quizzically.

"It's really extremely interesting. Keep an eye out for the way people look at each other across the table. Especially Archer and Countess Wolenska. I always think it's the way people look at each other rather than what they actually say that tells the whole story."

Grace cocked an eyebrow. "Really? That's interesting."

"Don't you think that's true?"

Grace looked up at him. She didn't know what to make of this guy. He wasn't taking her hints and buzzing off, but he didn't seem to be hitting on her either. He actually seemed interested in what she had to say.

"I mean," the guy said, waving at the beach behind him, "everyone on a beach says one thing but really does another. A guy will tell his girlfriend that he'll love her forever, but if another woman walks by in a bikini, his eyes are all over her. Isn't that sort of a lie?"

Grace nodded. "I guess so." she said.

"Well, I wouldn't want to keep you from that dinner scene. It's just that I've been in this town for three or four weeks and haven't had a good conversation with a single person. I thought people here would be reading and talking about books. I guess I was wrong."

Grace looked behind her at the beach. Volleyball players kicked up sand, Frisbees sliced through the air, heads bobbed in the water. "I guess you were," she said. "Don't you like to swim?"

"Not really," he answered.

"Well, what about sunbathing? Looks like you could use a little exposure," Grace said.

"Not with the ozone layer in its present tattered condition."

"Oh. Right." Grace sat back in her chair and looked him up and down. "Then why *are* you here?"

"I was under the impression that I might get some work as a tutor," he explained.

"Here? In Ocean City?"

"I have to spend the summer here at my parents' condo," he sighed. "They wouldn't let me do another summer session at school."

"That's a shame," Grace said earnestly.

"Yeah. I know. They had an awesome curriculum planned this summer. Greek tragedies and

102

Thomas Aquinas."

"And what is this mighty institution, may I ask?"

"St. John's College. Have you heard of it?"

"Where the Great Books program originated," Grace said.

"Wow. Not too many people even know we exist. So, anyway, I figured tutoring, it's what I'm good at, it's what I know, so . . . there we are."

"Nope," Grace said. "You're nowhere with that plan. Not much studying going on here in O.C. other than Babe Watching one-oh-one."

"Yeah, you're the first person I've seen reading anything other than *Muscle & Fitness* or *Seventeen*," he said.

"So what are you going to do with all your free time?" Grace asked, suddenly interested.

"Well, my parents decided that I'd spent enough time reading inside. They kicked me out about an hour ago and said that by the time I got back for dinner, I had to decide on something to do."

"And?" Grace asked, moving up to the edge of her seat.

"And nothing," he replied. "All there is here is sand and sky and water. Nothing to do at all."

"Nope. Dull, dull, dull."

"I suppose I can always spend the summer perfecting my chess game."

"Or earning some money," Grace said.

"What?"

Grace stood up. "Grace Caywood," she said, extending her hand.

"Wilton Groves," he said, taking her hand uncertainly.

Grace was happy to see that his handshake was firm. She expected a dead-fish handshake. She hated dead-fish handshakes.

"Well, Wilton, how's six dollars an hour to start, with a raise in two weeks if it works out?" Grace said smiling.

"But . . . what are you talking about?"

"I've been looking for someone to help me out at my beach stands and haven't found anyone I like or trust. And, well . . . I think I can trust you. Can I trust you?"

"Of course you can trust me, but—"

"Then you accept?" she interrupted him.

"Don't you want me to go away and think about it?"

"Your parents may not want you to sit home and read, but I'll *pay* you to read, and all you have to do is sit here and keep an eye on things. Do you really need to think about it?"

Wilton pursed his lips. "I guess not."

Grace was beaming. One problem solved. "Then why think?" she said.

EIGHT

Justin fell back against the enormous king-size bed, clutching his heart.

"I feel sorry for her too, Kate," he cried at the ceiling. "But I can't believe you're actually suggesting this!"

"But, Justin, she's alone. She has no money. She has no friends. She's stuck here. And she needs to get exactly where we're going. Don't you think that's a bizarre coincidence?"

"It is a bizarre coincidence, and that's all it is. She's not coming with us," Justin said. "She said she'd find a way to get there, and she will."

"Why can't it be with us?" Kate demanded.

"Why does it have to be with us?" Justin asked.

"Don't you believe in fate? We're in a position to help her out. Wouldn't you feel bad just leaving her behind when you know we could do something really helpful for her?"

"Yes, I believe in fate," Justin said. "I was fated to be with you. We were fated to be together. You and me. Just the *two* of us."

"Oh! You sound so callous," Kate cried, throwing a pillow at his head.

"Kate, this girl is not our responsibility. I don't want to share our time together with someone else. I can't believe you. One sob story and you're ready to throw away the possibility of what this trip could be for us. For you and me."

"But, Justin," Kate implored, "it's not just that I feel sorry for her. She may be a total klutz, but she did say she knows how to sail."

"So what?" Justin said. "Let her find another boat. A bigger boat, with more than two other people, one of whom hasn't been trying for two years to get his girlfriend—the woman he loves—on a boat with him, in the middle of the ocean, *alone!*"

"Justin, I understand why you're saying no. The idea of being alone with you is wonderful to me."

"But the reality doesn't cut it?" Justin said angrily.

"No, Justin. You know that's not the problem. I didn't follow you all the way to the

Bahamas just for an idea. It's the idea versus the reality of being on a boat in the middle of the ocean that I'm starting to worry about."

"You don't trust me?" Justin turned away, a hurt look in his eyes.

"Justin," Kate cried, exasperated. "It's not you I don't trust. It's me. And life. And the weather. I was really sick on the boat yesterday and today. I didn't admit to you before how awful I really felt. But I *really felt awful.*"

Kate walked over to the balcony and stood staring out at the moonlight on the water.

"I'm scared I'll feel that awful the whole time," she said softly. "And what if it gets worse instead of better?"

"Kate," Justin said from behind her, "I'll still love you if you get seasick."

"I know," Kate said, sighing, "but it's not just that. What if I'm too sick to help? What if you really need my help, or something worse—you get sick, and I have to sail by myself. I'm just not ready. I'm not that good. I don't even think I'm competent."

"You're competent, Kate," Justin said quickly. "You're competent in everything you do."

"What if sometime during our trip we get bad weather?" she went on, ignoring him. "What then? What if there's another storm like the one you were caught in with Grace? What if the same thing happens? I thought you were dead once, and I could barely stand it. What if something happened and I couldn't help you, I couldn't get the boat to you, I couldn't—"

He caught her from behind and turned her to him, holding her tightly.

"Kate, Kate," he said softly in her ear as she clutched him. "Is this the same woman who faced down a hurricane by herself?" Justin asked, lifting her chin and looking into her eyes, reminding her of the time she'd been caught out in that terrible storm. "You survived Hurricane Barbara, remember?"

"But I'm serious about this," Kate said softly. "I'm not suggesting it to avoid being with you. Of course we won't be alone, just the two of us. But there are so many advantages to asking her along. First, we get a good, experienced first mate. And second, we do a good, kind thing for a girl who needs help and a few friends."

Justin sighed deeply. "That's not so many. That's just two. And, anyway, where will she sleep? There's no room in our cabin."

"Justin, we can put a little cot in the galley, can't we?" Kate said softly. "I want to help her."

"Always saving the world," he answered, his voice resigned. "That's why I love you."

Kate kissed him on the cheek. "Does that mean yes?"

"Yes," Justin agreed, defeated. "That means yes. There's barely room to walk in the galley, but there's room for a cot, I guess. Today is Allegra Wolfe's lucky day. And she doesn't even know it."

The next day, back in her tiny room, Allegra tested out her glasses once more before throwing them carelessly into a chair. She pulled her brilliant red hair back into a messy ponytail, then took out a small duffel bag and started gathering her things together.

All in all, she thought the previous evening had gone well. So well, in fact, that she was sure she'd be seeing Kate in a little while.

Allegra sat back on her bed and sighed, forcing herself to calm down and think everything through again. It was all going according to plan. Kate was nice and easy. A pushover. Allegra had known right away how to play her. She was sure Kate was ready to invite her along. It would all depend on how convincing the young woman could be with her boyfriend.

Justin. Yes, he'd been difficult. Allegra smiled. But what a pleasant surprise he'd turned out to be. He was gorgeous. And sexy. And harder to reach.

Kate was bookish, but Justin was smart. Allegra knew she'd have to be careful around him. He was already suspicious about his boat. Allegra knew that from his visit to Chernak. She'd have to play down her interest in the *Kate*.

And how sweet that was, Allegra thought. He'd named the boat after his girlfriend. She gave a soft, menacing chuckle.

He obviously wasn't interested in extra company. But too bad for him, Allegra thought, because she was definitely interested. Interested in becoming more than just extra company.

Just hang out here a while longer, Allegra told herself, propping her feet on the railing of the little balcony off her tiny room. *She's going to come. I'm sure she's going to come. They're leaving tomorrow—she just has to come today, and finally, finally, I'll have put one over on Trevor, that bastard . . .* She sat flipping through a magazine without seeing it, keeping both eyes on the street below.

Kate made her way slowly through the marketplace. Still, even after so many days, she couldn't help but marvel at the noise, the smells, the activity that went on at the various stalls of the market.

Besides the expected areas for selling food—all kinds of interesting and beautiful fresh fruits and vegetables, as well as stacks of fish and barrels of various seafood—there were places set aside for local arts and crafts, plants, even animals and exotic birds.

She dodged bicycles, carts, and mopeds on the side streets until she saw the dingy hostel where Allegra had said she was staying. A figure was waving to her from a balcony on the third floor. Kate lifted her hand to her eyes to shade them from the sun and saw a flash of red hair. Allegra.

Kate smiled and waved in response. Just as she was about to drop her hand from her eyes, she saw Allegra turn away, pick something up off a table, and thrust her hand to her face. The sun glinted, two piercing stabs of light that blinded Kate for a moment until Allegra turned her head again. Of course, Kate remembered with a smile. Those thick glasses.

By the time she'd climbed the stairs to Allegra's floor, Allegra was waiting for her in the hallway, an excited grin on her face.

She really is so lonely, Kate thought.

"Hi, Kate!" Allegra cried. "It's so nice of you to come and visit. I mean . . . it's so nice to see a friendly face, you know? I was thinking of getting some lunch. Would you like to join me?"

"Um, sure, I think." Kate smiled. "But I have to get back to Justin and the boat soon. I really just came by to talk. And to ask you something."

"Oh." Allegra's face fell a bit, but she forced a quick smile. "Well, do you want to come in? It's not much, my room," Allegra said apologetically as she stepped aside, "but it's all I could find on such short notice."

Kate walked past her into the tiny room. There was a single bed in the corner. More a cot than a bed, really. And a rusty sink against the opposite wall. One worn-out stuffed chair. A low, wobbly table. And barely enough floor space to navigate in.

"But at least there's the little balcony," Allegra added as though reading Kate's mind. "I mean, I can't expect to have luxury accommodations. And, anyway, it's much better to spend most of the day outside. The beach here is more luxurious than even the nicest hotel room, don't you think?" Allegra pushed her glasses back onto her nose and smiled.

Kate looked around, not quite sure what to do with herself.

"Oh, I'm sorry." Allegra blushed, touching Kate lightly on the shoulder and pushing her back. "Please sit down. You take the chair. I'll sit on the bed."

Allegra moved toward the bed and banged her shin on the low table. She stepped back quickly and scraped her foot on one of the bed's metal legs.

"Ouch." She grimaced as she finally dropped down.

"Safe!" Kate said, laughing.

Allegra tried a smile.

"Listen," Kate began, "I just came by to tell you that Justin and I are leaving tomorrow, heading back to O.C."

"Really?" Allegra asked, her face falling a little. "I was hoping you might be around for a few days. Just to go sight-seeing with and stuff." She reached down to rub the sore spot on her shin. "But, anyway, that's great for you. You'll have a wonderful time sailing, I bet."

"Well," Kate admitted, "I'm not so sure about that. It's the thing I wanted to talk to you about. I'm really not the best sailor, and I'm a little nervous about being first mate. Now, I know"— Kate held up her hand to keep Allegra from speaking—"that you're going to think you forced us into offering, but it's not that way. Justin and I were wondering if you'd like to sail with us, that is, as long as you can be ready to leave tomorrow."

"S-sail with you?" Allegra stammered. "Do you mean it? Oh, no." She shook her head. "I can't do it. I'm sorry, I just can't."

"But why?" Kate asked. "You need a ride home, and we're going there. What better solution could there be?"

"I just couldn't take advantage that way . . . it's just not right . . . you have no choice really but to ask because you're both such nice people but—"

"Allegra," Kate cut her off. "We want you to come. You'll be a real help, actually, and it'll ease my mind a lot knowing that there's at least one other person onboard who knows how to handle a boat. Please, don't say no. We wouldn't offer if we didn't want to."

"Well." Allegra pulled nervously on her ponytail, and Kate saw how it always ended up lopsided. "Well . . . I want to . . . but I just want to be sure. . . ."

"Be sure, Allegra." Kate smiled. "It will be great. As long as you can put up with us and our other passenger."

"What other passenger?" Allegra suddenly snapped.

Kate looked at her with surprise. "Just Mooch, Justin's dog," she explained, surprised at Allegra's hostile reaction.

"Oh!" Allegra's face instantly softened. "Great! A dog. I love dogs, actually."

"Good," Kate said, "because he'll probably end up sleeping with you. And he's a real blanket hog."

Allegra grinned. "I really appreciate it, Kate. Really I do. I'll be great. I promise I won't get in the way."

"Well, don't make any promises you can't keep," Kate joked. "It's a pretty small boat."

"I'm much better on the water," Allegra said eagerly. "I told you that. And I won't break anything."

"Okay, okay." Kate nodded, heading for the door. "I've got to go get ready. So why don't you meet us at the marina tomorrow morning? About nine, I guess."

Allegra ran up and gave her a quick hug. "Thanks so much, Kate. You guys are the best."

"Just wait till we're out at sea." Kate grinned. "You may not think we're so great after living with us."

"Oh, no," Allegra cried happily. "I know I won't change my mind. This is really going to be great."

As soon as Kate closed the door, Allegra whirled around and kicked the wall.

"Fool!" Allegra hissed, cursing herself. "If you can't keep it together for a couple of young teenaged lovers, how can you possibly expect to beat Chernak!"

She stormed around the tiny room hitting and smacking everything in her way to release her tension. Finally she went to the little mirror that hung crookedly over the rusty sink that passed for a bathroom. She eyed herself cruelly.

"Remember," she snarled at the reflection in the mirror, "the gawky talk and thick glasses are an *act!* And if you want to make this work"—her eyes narrowed to slits—"it's an act you have to remember to play! Don't forget the glasses like that again. Or it'll be over."

Mooch was whining and shaking, leaning over the edge of the boat toward the dock that was pulling farther away by the second.

"Is he okay?" Allegra worried.

"Oh, he's all right," Justin assured her. "He's just realizing he had his last opportunity to . . . well, to relieve himself on firm ground. Mooch loves to sail, but unfortunately there's no sand around here to cover up after himself. He's actually very shy, you know."

"Oh." Allegra blushed.

"Why don't you go put your stuff belowdeck?" Justin suggested. "We're not really into a strong wind here yet, so Kate can handle it, I'm sure."

Allegra nodded, then disappeared down the tiny stairs with her duffel.

"So?" Kate smiled at Justin. "Are you excited? We're moving." She turned and waved good-bye to the island behind them.

"You're silly."

"Only on a boat."

"That's why it took you so long to come with me," Justin said somberly. "You didn't want me to see this chink in your armor."

Kate laughed and tossed back her head. "I feel great so far. No sickness for me!" She moved behind Justin and laced her arms around his stomach. "So?"

"So what?"

"So what about Allegra?" Kate whispered. "Are you still mad at me?"

Justin sighed. "Well, she is a good sailor," he admitted. "I guess that's something to ease the mind. But . . ."

"But what?"

"Well, it'll be a good trip," Justin said, "but it won't be quite the honeymoon I envisioned."

Allegra came back on deck and swung under the boom, moving to the rear of the boat and grabbing the sail line.

Kate glanced back at her and then did a double take. Something was different, Kate could see right away. But it took her a second to figure out exactly what it was. Allegra was standing comfortably, which in and of itself seemed strange. Kate was used to seeing her on the verge of toppling over. But Allegra *had* promised she wasn't clumsy when sailing.

Kate looked at her again. She was still wearing her baggy T-shirt and long shorts. And her thick glasses sat squarely in the center of her face. Ahh, that was it. She'd taken her hair down from its ponytail. Loose, it now fluttered behind her in the wind, catching the sunlight and glinting a rainbow of deep auburns and reds. It was gorgeous.

"Wow." Kate sighed jealously. "You should wear your hair down all the time. It's really beautiful."

Allegra raised a hand to her head awkwardly, self-consciously.

"Do you really think so?" she asked hesitantly. "I just like the way it feels in the wind. I don't think much about how it looks."

"Well, it looks great," Kate said. "Don't you think so, Justin?" she added, poking him.

"Sure." He nodded. "It looks nice."

Allegra smiled and blushed.

"I think I'm going to go down for a minute," Kate announced, and as she passed by Justin, she leaned over and whispered to him, "she's sweet. Be nice to her. She needs a little ego boosting, and a few words from a hunk like yourself would do her good."

"Why do women always do this to their boyfriends?" Justin whispered back, shaking his head. "You're asking me to flirt with her? How would you have felt if I'd done it *without* your permission?" He raised his eyebrow.

"Okay, you win." Kate shrugged. "I just feel sorry for her."

Kate went down the stairs into the tight galley below. As soon as she was out of sight, she leaned against the wall and closed her eyes. Boy, she'd really lied up there. She wasn't feeling great at all, and the person she was feeling sorry for was herself. She felt sick. Much worse than the queasiness she'd had on their little shakedown runs. This was building up into something truly nauseating.

She stumbled across the little galley to the small cot where Allegra's bag lay. As she went to sit, she felt a wave of sickness and reached out, knocking the bag onto the floor. She bent over to retrieve it, but when she pulled it up, everything fell out of the open zipper.

Kate sighed, her head pounding and her stomach doing flip-flops. She reached down and started grabbing the rolled-up clothes, shoving them haphazardly back into the bag. But suddenly she slowed. She was holding something very soft. And very sensual. She looked down and saw a deep-green silk teddy in her lap. Edged in black lace.

I know this thing, Kate realized immediately. *Victoria's Secret, page seven. The thing I couldn't bring myself to order.*

She reached down again and pulled up a

119

fire-engine red camisole. Then a racy bikini. She held the bottoms up in front of her. Were these the bottoms? Kate thought. It looked like two pieces of string tangled together. Kate turned it to a different angle. Nope. Definitely no triangles anywhere. This wasn't the top half of anything. But you could hardly call it a bottom half. It looked as if it would show much more than half a bottom.

Quickly Kate grabbed the rest of Allegra's clothes and stuffed them back into the bag. Then she sat back slowly and rested her head against the wall. She felt uncomfortable, as if she'd just been spying on someone. As if she'd just found out a dangerous secret. But no, she decided. Nothing dangerous. Just odd. Very odd.

She's so . . . awkward, Kate thought. *She seems so shy. But those aren't the clothes of a shy person. No way.*

NINE

"Where do you want me to put the ice?" David asked, standing in the kitchen doorway with an enormous Styrofoam cooler in his arms.

Grace looked around the kitchen. Stacks of colored paper plates were piled on the table. Plastic silverware lay scattered on the counters.

"Well," she said, "there's no room in here. Let's see, there's going to be chip and dip in the living room, movies downstairs . . ."

"Grace," Marta said from behind her, "give the guy a break. He's straining."

"Oh, that's okay," David said good-humoredly from the doorway, the veins in his arms indeed popping. "This is just one small way of making me suffer for leaving her."

"What?" Grace demanded. "You won't allow me any fun? For all intents and purposes, in less

121

than eighteen hours I'll practically be a widow."

Marta grimaced, knocking quickly on the kitchen table. "Don't joke like that about somebody who's going up in a fighter plane."

"Okay, sorry," Grace said. "I can't help it. That's my true nature. You all were deceived into *thinking* I was a nicer person because I was happy for a time. But now the real me is back."

"You are a nicer person," David said.

"And I'm going to miss you very much," Grace snapped, turning away and wiping her eyes, "so let me be nasty, just for tonight. I know it's stupid, but it's a very popular defense mechanism. All the best people do it, you know."

"Why don't you put that on the patio?" Marta said to David. He smiled gratefully and headed outside.

Just then the doorbell rang.

"Come in!" Grace shouted.

It rang again. And again.

"I'll get it," Marta said. "Must be someone we don't know."

She wheeled back into the kitchen a second later with a quizzical expression on her face. Wilton, actually wearing a jacket and tie, was right behind her, a box of After Eight dinner mints in his hand.

"Grace?" Marta questioned.

"Oh, hi, Wilton. This is my newest employee," she explained to Marta.

"Wilton Groves," Wilton said, sticking out his hand.

"Marta Salgado," Marta replied, struggling to keep a straight face.

"And what do you do, Miss Salgado?" Wilton began, as if by rote.

"Oh, you don't have to bother getting to know her," Grace quipped. "She's moving out."

"Okay." Wilton nodded, obviously relieved. He turned and left the kitchen.

Grace and Marta looked at each other and burst out laughing.

"What was that?" Marta sputtered.

"My new employee," Grace repeated.

"I heard that part. I mean, where does he come from?"

"Not this planet, that's for sure," Grace answered.

Where was he? Chelsea wondered, checking her watch again. She knew she shouldn't have left him alone. He'd promised he'd be right behind her. Just one scene to finish, he'd said. Five minutes at the most.

One scene, which had apparently taken the last four hours, Chelsea fumed. She couldn't believe he was bagging out on her like this. Not just her, but their friends, too. Granted it wasn't really a major farewell party for Marta, but she *was* moving uptown, and in a place like Ocean City that meant they might not see her for the rest of the summer. But David was leaving the country. And Connor couldn't bother to show up and say good-bye?

Chelsea paced the foyer again, debating about whether or not to go get him. Then the door flew open, and Chelsea had to leap back to avoid being pounded into the wall. Connor rushed in, grabbing handfuls of refreshments as he whirled through the house. He shoved some nacho chips into his mouth, took a swig of soda, clapped David on the back, and waved to Marta.

"Great," he said with his mouth full. "Great party, glad I could make it. Farewell, David, it's been a pleasure knowing you. You've opened my stomach to a new ethnic gastronomy—borscht, latkes, bagels with lox. Don't mind me if I write about you someday. Very inspiring. And please wear your seat belt. Fly straight, fly high, and fly fast—especially if someone is after you. And, Marta, here's my advice: Just because you buy different-colored toothbrushes, don't think that *means* anything at all. When it's late and he's tired, he'll reach for the nearest one. Bear with it, because surely it's the thought of fresher breath that matters."

He started to turn away when Chelsea caught him by the shoulders.

"Connor!" she snapped. "Where are you going?"

"Going? Going? To hell in a handbasket if I don't get back to work, that's where!" he exclaimed.

"You're leaving already?" Chelsea cried. "That little speech is all you can afford? That's all you have to say?"

"Look, Chels," Connor replied indignantly. "That editor called me this afternoon. He was asking about the rest of the book. He says he's anxious to read it, and the sooner the better before he forgets what he *has* read. So to answer your question, yes, I do have other things to say. But I can't say them here. Got to get back to the pages. Can't say something I'll forget by the time I get home. Got to save up the good stuff, you know."

"You've got to save up the good stuff?" Chelsea shrieked. "I can't believe you. Aren't we your friends? And am I your wife? Nobody in this house deserves any of your 'good stuff'?"

"Chels." Connor dropped his voice and looked around. "I hate to point this out, but you're really making a fool of yourself."

"I'm making a fool of myself? No, Connor.

That'd be your job right now. You are acting like a fool. Very much so—"

"Listen," Connor interrupted, "I'd love to stay. Really I would." He smiled quickly and nodded, the sentiment almost reaching his eyes. "But I can't. Gotta get back to work."

"You've got to talk to me is what you have to do!" Chelsea cried.

"Okay, okay." Connor pulled her out of the living room, dragged her to the laundry room, and slammed the door. He was bouncing on the balls of his toes, ready at any second to start running.

"So what is it you want to say? And Chels"— he glanced at his watch—"can you make it quick? Because I've really got to go."

Grace couldn't make out any of the words, but for the next fifteen minutes Chelsea's muffled voice rose and fell in the background as the party went on.

Finally the laundry-room door opened and Connor fell out, looking dazed and frightened. He moved shakily to the front door.

"No more!" he cried. "No more!"

Chelsea was right on his tail. "Yes, more," she threatened. "You can't act this way. It's not right. It's not fair—"

"Fair? Who cares about fair? My career is in

your hands, and all you want me to do is mingle? I'm a writer," he cried, "an artist, can't you see that?"

"I can see that you're something," Chelsea said, backing him out the front door, "but I don't think I'd use the words 'writer' and 'artist' at this point."

"What would you use?" Connor asked, aghast.

"Well, how about—"

The door slammed closed behind them. Grace shook her head.

"Wow, some farewell party this is turning out to be," Marta said.

"Tell me about it." Grace rolled her eyes.

"They just got back together," Marta said. "I wonder what's wrong."

"You'll find out soon enough. That's what happens when you move in with someone."

"Hmm, not a very good omen, is it?"

"Not really," Grace agreed, wondering whether a beer would take away the headache that was coming on. She looked across the room and saw David talking and laughing with Dominic. Some farewell party. Her heart was breaking. This was the last night she'd have with David, and she couldn't bear to look at him. He looked so happy and excited. She sighed, knowing that was exactly how she'd looked when she'd left him last summer.

Dominic made his way over to Marta and leaned down to whisper something in her ear. Marta blushed and nodded. Grace watched her roll over to the couch to get her bag.

"Grace," she began, fishing her keys out of her purse, "I think we're going to head off now. Thanks for the party."

"My pleasure," Grace replied.

"No, it wasn't," Marta said knowingly, "but thanks anyway. I hope you realize this won't be the last you see of me. I'm keeping my keys."

"At least I'll know who to call for a spare."

"Just don't be surprised if I come over to take advantage of the easy beach access."

"You're always welcome." Grace leaned down and gave her a hug.

"And listen, about your new roommate—"

"You found somone? That's great."

"Don't you want to know who it is?" Marta asked slyly.

"I'm sure I'll find out soon enough. I trust you not to saddle me with a mass murderer or something."

"Okay." Marta smiled. "Your choice. Just don't say I didn't try to warn you."

David joined Grace on the front stoop as she waved good-bye. She closed the door and felt his arms circle her from behind. It felt so good to be held, she almost started crying.

"Grace?" His voice was soft as he turned her around. "Well, we're finally alone. Everyone's gone off to bed. Not a bad idea."

Grace looked into his brown eyes, and she could see the desire in them. *One last night,* she thought. *One last night.* Could she lie back and forget, even for a minute, that he was leaving?

David pulled her closer, but she shook her hand and pushed him back.

"I can't," she whispered.

"Grace?" he said softly. "I love you."

"I know," she replied, her voice catching. "But it's no good anymore. Not tonight. I can't do the farewell—"

"Don't say it," David interrupted, closing his eyes and resting his forehead on hers. "Please don't say it like that. That's not what I wanted."

"But that's how it feels," Grace replied. "I can't help it. I'm not as good at this as you were. I'm not graceful about having my heart broken. You can't stay, or I'll get even worse."

She pulled away from him.

"I don't want to be like this, David," she pleaded. "Not to you. But it's still the only way I know to protect myself. If you stay, I'll be terrible to you. And then after you go, I'll feel guilty about it forever."

"So you want me to go now?" he asked sadly.

She could only nod. She heard him pick up his helmet from the floor.

"I'm not leaving because I want to," David said softly. "Not tonight. And not tomorrow either. I *will* see you again," he said.

"Don't remember me like this," Grace whispered as David came up behind her. He leaned down and kissed her neck.

"I'll remember you every way," he promised.

Grace waited until the front door shut and she heard the sound of his motorcycle fade before she allowed herself to move. Then immediately she was moving and crying all at the same time. She swept past the debris of the party, bowls of chips and dip, empty pizza boxes, half-filled cans of soda, the tattered good-bye signs hanging at angles on the glass patio doors: "Tie One On in Taiwan (just kidding)" and "Watch Out! She's an Uptown Girl Now!"

The water was black. The beach was empty. Grace leaned on the railing and sobbed quietly for a while. She listened to the ocean roll in until she caught her breath, and, finally, she turned back to the house and headed up to bed.

"What are you doing here?" Grace cried out when she got to her room. She quickly tried to wipe the tears from her eyes.

Her new employee looked up from where he

crouched, on his knees in front of her small bookcase. All her books were spread out in little stacks around him.

"Why are you in my room?" Grace asked.

"I was just . . . organizing these for you."

"Organizing?" Grace repeated. "My books?"

"You know, alphabetically." Wilton looked back to the bookshelf.

"Can I ask why? Do you know what time it is?" Grace said. "Everyone's gone home. The party's over."

"I was up here, taking a look around—" Wilton began.

"Look, I know the party wasn't a total success, but you're saying it wasn't even as exciting as my bookshelf?" Grace commented, wiping at her eyes again.

"I'm not really a party person," Wilton admitted.

"No, really?" Grace feigned shock. "I couldn't tell."

"I'm not a party person," Wilton repeated, "but I am capable of discerning sarcasm when it's directed at me."

She smiled tightly and laughed. "Okay. Sorry."

Wilton shrugged. "Some things are important to some people. Parties aren't those things for me."

"Yeah, well, you're probably better off for

that." Grace nodded, remembering all too well when parties, and drinking, seemed to be the only two things that were important to her.

"Anyway," Wilton continued, "I was looking at your books, but I couldn't see what you had. I thought you didn't have even one book by Cervantes. I mean, who doesn't have *Don Quixote*? But I thought you didn't. We read that book at school last year. It's so lovely. I thought what a shame that you didn't know 'For Beauty in a virtuous Woman is but like a distant Flame, or a sharp-edg'd Sword, and only burns and wounds those who approach too near it.'"

"Is there any particular reason you picked that part?" Grace winced, turning away and pulling a tissue from the box by her bed.

"Excuse me?"

"Nothing," Grace said, turning back to him. "But, you see, I do have it." She pointed to a copy of *Don Quixote* lying at his feet. "I *have* that book. I've read it too," she said.

"I know," he answered. "But it was all the way on the bottom. I didn't see it right away. It should be near the top. So you can find it easily."

Grace pushed her hair back from her face and looked at him again. Was it really possible that he had no idea how ridiculous it was for him to be there in her room? Grace wondered. Did he really fail to see that her eyes were red and puffy from crying? Couldn't he see that she didn't want company now, of all times?

"Perhaps I haven't been looking for it. Did you consider that?" she snapped.

Wilton nodded and smiled crookedly. Then he turned back to her books. "But you really need some help with your library here," he went on, ignoring her remark.

"Really?" Grace sniffed. "I didn't know I was building one."

"Well, you should be," Wilton said. "Books are very important." He leaned down and skimmed the stacks of books with his hands. "They have all of life in them," he said reverently.

"Sure they do," Grace said coldly. "But you can also learn about life by living it. There's a lot to learn that way, too, Will. Don't knock the real world. It can give you just as much heartache as *Madame Bovary*. And you can't just close the book and walk away."

"It's 'Wilton,' not 'Will,'" he answered quietly.

Grace nodded and turned aside. *Of course*, she thought. Not "Will." She walked over to the open doorway and stepped out onto the balcony.

Was this a movie or what? She'd just been hostess to the most depressing party of her life. The man she loved was leaving her. All her friends were gone or going away. And there was a stranger in her bedroom adamantly set against a one-syllable version of his name.

"I'm just going to put them back," Wilton called out. "Since I've taken them out."

Grace nodded and sank into a chair. She listened to the sound of muttering and the soft whisper of books sliding into place. Every once in a while she heard his voice rise and fall rhythmically, reading or reciting passages he liked.

She had no idea how long he'd been there. The stars had shifted, she knew that much. It wasn't all that dark out anymore. Finally she heard him stand up.

"I'm done," he said softly. "Don't get up, I'll just let myself out."

"Fine," Grace replied, playing with the tissue in her hand.

"Good night, Grace," he said as he opened her bedroom door.

"Good night, Wilton-not-Will," she replied, leaning her head back and closing her tired eyes.

TEN

Chelsea stood outside the closed door to the back room and listened. She didn't hear anything and was a little worried. Connor hadn't slept in the same bed with her for two or three nights. Lying on the sheets alone, she'd heard nothing except the snapping of typewriter keys echoing through the house. And in the mornings she hadn't said anything more to him than "Want me to make you some breakfast?" or "Why don't you take a nap for just a *half* hour?" and he hadn't done anything more than grunt. Once she caught him sprawled on the floor underneath his desk like a homeless man sleeping in a cardboard box. Still, every time she went into the back room, the pile of pages he was calling *Beach Blanket Begorra* was getting bigger, growing like a misshapen plant.

But now she didn't hear anything. She knocked once and opened the door. The Connor she saw was a changed man. Unwashed, unshaven, he was walking around the room, gesturing in the air, murmuring snatches of dialogue to himself like a person suffering from multiple-personality disorder.

"Uh, Connor?" Chelsea said. "Hello?"

"Yeah, uh, hi, Chels," Connor said, then turned around and answered himself, translating everything, including real life, into fictional dialogue: "Hi, Connor, and how are you? Just fine, Chels. How was your day? Fine, Connor, and yours?"

"Connor!" Chelsea cried, shaking him by the shoulders.

"Oh, sorry, Chels. I'm just caught up in something here." Connor went back to his desk and didn't sit in the chair so much as collapse into it.

"You know," Chelsea said, rubbing his shoulders, "I don't think those editors in New York would mind if you took just a *few* days off. It would do you some good. Maybe you'd even feel like a human being again."

Connor shrugged her hands off him. "I don't want to feel human, Chels. I'm a writer writing. I'm *working*. No Washington. No human being. Nothing. Write. I've got to write." He tapped his temple. "It's all up here." Then he laid his hands on the typewriter. "I've got to get it all down here."

"Connor, you're talking like a Neanderthal," Chelsea said. "If this is artistic success, then I don't want it."

Connor turned around. "But I *do!*"

"But successful writers can be people, too," she said. "I've seen them interviewed. They shower in the morning. They work at their desks. They eat lunch. They work some more. Then they eat dinner. They hang out, maybe watch some bad TV or read a book. Then they brush their teeth. And then, Connor, they go—to—bed."

"Don't mock me," Connor said, his voice brimming with anger. "I don't have time for this."

"You don't have time for anything. You don't even have time to go down to D.C. tomorrow and see your own goddaughter. Your *goddaughter,* Connor, my cousin's brand-new baby girl."

"Well, people who have *talent,* Chelsea, can't always be expected to do all the silly things other people demand of them," Connor snapped.

"Why, you—" Chelsea seethed.

Connor stood up and held out his hands. "I'm sorry, Chels. I didn't mean *you.* I just meant—"

Chelsea was so angry she could hardly talk. "Why you self-important, conceited little—"

"Chelsea, I said I'm sorry! I didn't mean it. I meant—"

"I know what you meant, Connor. I know you think I'm just a minor little artist who does stupid little sketches. And that now I'm selling out and doing graphic stuff for a stupid little ad company. I know you think I have no talent and I'm wasting my time. You've always thought that."

"Chelsea, no. I never thought that. Never," Connor said, shaking his head.

He took a step toward her. Chelsea took another step back.

"Maybe you didn't realize you thought it," Chelsea said, "but obviously you do. Otherwise you never would have said it."

"Chels, that's not true—"

"Well, let me tell you something, Mr. Writer. I *am* talented. And my dream is not to do boardwalk sketches or work in an ad agency forever. I'm responsible. I have a *job,* because someone has to *work.* One day I'll do what you're doing, but I'll do it when I don't have to rely on someone else for support! That's what you had. You had my support. But you just kept pushing me away, pushing me away. Well, now you've pushed me too far. Now you'll see what it feels like to have no support. I'm going down to D.C.— by myself."

Chelsea headed for the door. "And you never know who I might run into," she tossed over her shoulder.

138

＊   ＊   ＊

Grace heard an incredibly intrusive noise from far off. Indescribable, it seemed designed particularly to annoy. It came closer, bleating by her head like a jet-sized mosquito. For the fifth time—or was it the sixth?—she sent her arm out of the dark coolness of her comforter to patrol her shelf for her alarm clock. Quiet. She felt the tension evaporate. More sleep. She needed just a little more sleep.

When was the last time she'd slept in?

"B.W. Before Wilton. Thank God for Wilton," she murmured, and rolled over. Today was day one, the year one, A.W. After Wilton. May it be a year of leisure, late mornings—

"And lonely nights," Grace moaned.

For the hundredth time she replayed in her mind the muted roar of David's motorcycle as he'd peeled out of her driveway the night before.

I shouldn't have let him go, she thought.

She closed her eyes and tried to picture him now, buckled into an air-force transport headed west over the United States, over the Pacific. At least a thousand miles away already, and getting farther away by the second. Was he thinking of her? Would he ever think of her?

"Who cares?" she said, sitting up in bed. Today was day one.

Grace's heart began to pound. She eyed her clock.

"Eleven fifteen!" she exclaimed. "Wow, I really needed that."

The house was utterly quiet. She could hear the roof creaking, expanding with the late-morning sun. The ceiling groaned, a settling noise. She could hear her own heartbeat. The house didn't feel quiet so much as it felt empty, hollow, abandoned.

Marta was out of the house, she thought. Chelsea was out of town. David was gone, out of her life, maybe for good. Her mother was gone, too, definitely for good. Her heart felt like the big empty house she lived in. A shell within a shell.

"Well, there's Roan and Bo, at least," she thought.

Grace made her way downstairs to the kitchen and started spooning heaps of coffee into the machine. She put in the water, flicked the switch, and waited.

Then she heard knocking. Pounding. She eyed the coffee machine.

Then she heard the floorboards creaking. She cocked her head and decided it must have been coming from Marta's old room. "Must have forgotten something," she muttered, and bounded down the steps.

"Marta?" she asked, turning the corner into her room. "What did you for—"

What she saw wasn't Marta but a muscular, golden back, a gorgeous pair of calves, and a pair of red Beach Patrol shorts.

"Uh, hello?"

The most beautiful man she'd ever seen turned around to face her. She made the judgment right away. It made her angry. He looked like all those pea-brains who stared down her bikini top at the beach. But different. He didn't look like a jerk.

"Excuse me?" the man said. He had a sweet, young voice. If he hadn't been sprouting all those muscles, she would have described him as angelic.

As his eyes traveled over Grace's body, clearly visible in her clingy silk robe, he turned crimson from the neck up, like a thermometer.

"No, excuse *me*," Grace said, clutching the top of her robe around her neck. "Who are you?"

"I'm your new roommate."

"My what? . . . Uh, I mean, *good.* If Marta picked you, I'm sure we'll get along fine. My name's Grace Caywood." Grace held out her hand.

"I'm Carr. Carr . . . um," he blushed even more deeply, looking everywhere but at her.

"Carr . . . what?"

"Carr Savett," Carr said, grasping her petite hand in his enormous one.

Perfect grip, Grace thought. *Firm but sensitive.* A strangely familiar sensation ran up her spine, one she wasn't ready to identify—at least not yet.

"So," she said. "What's that you're holding?"

"Oh, uh, just a . . ." The photograph slipped from his fingers. Both of them bent for it at once and knocked heads.

"Ouch. Sorry," Grace said.

"No, please, it's my fault," Carr said apologetically. "Are you all right? Here, sit here."

"Thanks," Grace said, settling into a chair.

Just as Carr swept the photograph away, Grace got a quick look. It was Carr and another woman, short blond hair, clean, all-American face, strong arms. Behind her, in the distance, was a silo of some sort, and behind that was a pale sea of wheat.

"Pretty," Grace said, nodding at the photograph. "Who's that, your sister?" she asked, failing to cover up the hope in her voice.

"Uh, no," Carr said, sticking the picture back into his bag. He was blushing again. "I don't have any sisters."

"Oh," Grace said, her eyes roaming the room. "So . . . best buddy from high school?"

"Sort of," Carr replied uncomfortably. "Actually, she's my . . . um . . . girlfriend, Jody."

For some reason a chilly wind blew through Grace.

"Oh," she said, and quickly stood up. "Well, let me leave you so you can get settled. I'm sure you'd like to get that picture up on the wall."

"Well," Carr said, looking hopelessly lost, "I . . . I guess I should unpack. But it was excellent—I mean, nice—to meet you. Grace, right?"

"Right. Grace. As in 'amazing.'"

Carr looked confused.

"That was a joke, Carr," Grace explained.

"Oh."

"Uh, Carr?"

"Yeah, Grace?"

"Where are you from?" Grace pointed at the photo lying on the bed. "I mean, all that wheat."

"Kansas," he said. "A small town outside Lawrence. You wouldn't have heard of it."

"Kansas," Grace said, nodding as if that made everything clear.

Just as the train was pulling into Union Station in Washington, D.C., Chelsea propped herself up in the little bathroom and leaned against the door for support. She was frantically applying last-minute touch-ups to her face. She always dressed well and wore plenty of makeup around her family. Her mother was a strong advocate of fashion and cosmetics, no doubt because those companies had the biggest advertising accounts with her magazine.

Repainted, tucked in, and smiling, Chelsea admired her outfit in the mirror: a tight linen skirt that accentuated her curves, and a loose silk blouse that boldly accented the rich color of her skin.

"Yup," she said to herself, smacking her lips to blot her lipstick. "You don't look bad for an old married woman."

She stepped off the train filled with anticipation. She looked right and left along the platform. Passengers and porters, but no family. She headed for the taxi stand across the station's gargantuan atrium. Dabbing her forehead with the back of her hand, Chelsea realized she'd forgotten how awful Washington summers were, hot and sticky, like breathing water. But stopping to admire the magnificent architecture of the building, she also remembered how majestic Washington was, and how tiny and sort of insignificant Ocean City felt by comparison.

Suddenly her bags were grabbed out of her hands, and a long, strong arm appeared around her waist.

"B.D.!" Chelsea called, whirling around and circling her brother's neck with her arms.

"Whoa, now," B.D. said. "You're going to break my neck."

"I'm sorry," Chelsea said, smiling with embarrassment and smoothing her skirt and blouse. She stepped back and admired her brother, who was wearing his dress whites from the naval academy.

Chelsea whistled, looking him up and down. "Well, now, don't you look fine. Your whites are so bright, you almost look like a ghost!"

"Chelsea, you remember Antonio, don't you?" B.D. said, pointing behind her. Chelsea took a deep breath and turned around.

Antonio was exactly as she remembered him, tall and powerful, with a beautifully sculpted face and perfect posture. And all of it was accentuated by his dress whites, giving him an air of composure and dignity.

He took her hand in both of his and looked into her face.

"It's been a long time, Chelsea," he said softly.

"That uniform suits you, Mr. Palmer," Chelsea said, smiling. "I'm not surprised." She reached up and pecked his cheek. "It's good to see you," she said demurely. She squeezed his hands. "I can't tell you how sorry I was when I heard about your mother."

Mrs. Palmer had been a logistics-and-supply sergeant for the marines, stationed in a rear-base support area during the Persian Gulf war. She was supposed to be safe, but early one morning a stray Scud had landed in her compound, turning her dormitory into an inferno. There were no survivors.

Chelsea remembered Mrs. Palmer as a kind, beautiful woman who supported anything her son did, so long as it was honorable and in keeping with the rules of the Church. Through high school Antonio never lied, never broke his curfew or disobeyed her in any way. He and his father worshiped his mother, and Antonio had told Chelsea when they were in tenth grade that he wanted to join the marines and be just like his mother.

Antonio cast his eyes on the floor and forced a smile. "Thank you. She'd be glad I'm doing what I'm doing," he said.

"She wouldn't only be glad," Chelsea affirmed, gripping Antonio's hands even tighter. "She'd be proud. You couldn't honor her in any better way."

Antonio looked up. His face seemed to brighten. "Thanks, Chelsea. I could always rely on you to—"

"All right, break it up," B.D. said, stepping between them. "The temperature in here rose about ten degrees once you two set eyes on each other. You better stop right now before that carrot-topped Irishman of yours catches sight of you mooning like two high-school freshmen. I've heard how messy those guys can get, but I don't want to have to see it up close and personal."

"Yeah," Antonio said, twisting around, "I'm looking forward to meeting your husband."

"Where is he, Chels?" B.D. asked, sweeping his eyes around the station.

Chelsea looked down at the ground. "He couldn't make it," she said, barely above a whisper.

B.D.'s broad smile flattened and his eyes clouded over. This was just what Chelsea was afraid of. Her family was so overprotective. She had to give them a good reason for Connor's absence, otherwise they'd never forget—or forgive—it.

"There's a good reason," Chelsea said quickly.

"Uh-huh," B.D. said, crossing his arms. "Missing his own goddaughter's christening?"

"Don't be like that, B.D. Connor had some . . . uh . . . good news. It's good news for both of us. But I wanted to tell everyone at the same time."

"All I can say is that it better be good," B.D. warned.

"It's good, all right," Chelsea said, turning around to get her bags. But she found her nose pressed into a wall of white cloth.

"Oh, sorry," Antonio said, catching Chelsea by the arms. "You okay?"

Chelsea laughed and laid her arm on Antonio's. "I'm fine."

Am I flirting? she asked herself. *I'm a married woman. Married women can't flirt.*

Then she pictured Connor bent over his typewriter, pecking away. Working harder than she'd thought capable. That was good. But then she remembered how he'd hardly even raised his head to say good-bye when she'd said she was leaving. He hadn't even noticed the way she was dressed.

Chelsea gritted her teeth with anger.

Is this why I wore this outfit? she thought, taking her brother's arm as they walked toward the parking lot. In the corner of her eye she saw Antonio trying hard not to throw admiring glances her way. But he was failing. And as she walked arm in arm between her two hunky military escorts, a not-so-hidden part of her didn't feel the least bit sorry. In fact, she was actually enjoying herself.

ELEVEN

They were well out to sea now, with no possibility of turning back. There was a nice, steady wind pushing them through the water. At least Justin and Allegra would have said it was a nice wind.

But Kate didn't think the wind was nice at all. Even though it was guiding the boat along and filling the billowy sail, it was also turning the ocean into what Kate thought of as an enormous, wet cheese grater.

The boat was the hunk of cheddar, sliding across the choppy ocean, dipping in and out of all the sharp little holes—and Kate was all of the little pieces of cheese that were getting left behind. Or, rather, all the little pieces of cheese that were getting left behind were coming from her. Though they didn't look like cheese.

Unfortunately, they looked a lot like the chips and salsa she'd snacked on about an hour ago. And she couldn't help but notice she hadn't chewed her food all that well.

Kate moaned again and pressed her face against the side of the boat. She was really sick now. What had been coming on slowly since the beginning of the trip had finally forced her to the side of the boat.

Whatever she'd thought about it before, Kate now knew that the ocean was just much too huge. She raised her head slowly and looked at it.

Endless. Blue and endless.

"Help," she whispered softly to the horizon.

Kate longed to get away from the railing. She was getting cramps in her legs, and the wind and salt water were beginning to chap her skin. But there was nowhere else to go. Every time she tried to sit or lie down, she felt dizzy enough to pass out, and a fresh new wave of nausea would hit her.

"I don't understand," Kate moaned. "There's nothing left in me. Why don't I feel better yet?"

"It's mental, Kate," Justin said from somewhere nearby.

"What do you mean 'mental'!" Kate shrieked. "I'm not making this up. Just take a look back there if you don't believe me." Kate pointed behind them. "There's a trail of half-digested food leading all the way back to the Bahamas. If anyone is trying to follow us, they sure won't have any trouble."

"What did you say?" Allegra's voice was squeaky. "Is someone following us?"

"No," Justin answered. "Kate's just making a joke."

"At least I still have my sense of humor," Kate said. "I've left all my internal organs behind."

"I know, baby," Justin soothed, and she felt his hand rubbing her back. "I didn't mean you were imagining your seasickness. I meant that you're sick because you're looking too closely at one thing in front of you, and that's telling your body that you aren't moving. But of course you really are."

"So?"

"So your brain is receiving *mixed messages*. That's why you don't feel well."

"So what can I do?" Kate whined. "This whole thing is full of potholes!" Kate gestured to the bumpy ocean. "It's worse than the worst street in New York City."

"Just keep your eyes on the horizon, honey," Justin suggested. "Stop staring at the hull and get a view of the big picture. And take some deep breaths. I guarantee you'll feel much better in a little while."

"How quick a little while?" Kate moaned.

"You'll know when you're better," Justin replied, smoothing back her hair.

"Oh, no, Justin, what if I have to stay out here all night, tied to the railing, staring at the moon? I won't be able to move."

And Allegra and Justin will be down in the cabin together. Alone!

Kate suddenly realized that puking over the railing was *not* a romantic image. And she didn't want the image of Justin and Allegra alone together to turn into one.

"I'll be fine by tonight," she yelled quickly and loudly. "In fact, I'm feeling much better already."

"Good, baby, don't worry." He leaned down and whispered in her ear. "I'll rub your tummy and make you feel better, Katie. I'll put a washcloth on your head, okay?"

She nodded and smiled. Then she dropped her head. *Mmmm, I love him,* she thought.

"You know, seasickness is nothing to be ashamed of, Kate," Allegra offered.

Kate clutched at the railing before turning to smile stiffly at Allegra, who stood over her, her hair blowing freely in the wind, and a sleek and stylish swimsuit accentuating her long, slender figure. *So no more dowdy shorts,* Kate noticed wryly.

*And she's really stressing that word "ashamed,"
isn't she?* Kate thought.

"You know even Admiral Nelson suffered from
seasickness," Allegra offered sweetly, as though
Kate could take any comfort from that thought.

"You mean I'm just like Admiral Nelson?" Kate
smirked. "That's just super lucky for me then,
isn't it?"

"Look," Allegra continued kindly, ignoring
the bitchiness in Kate's voice. "I know just how
you feel. On land I'm a complete klutz. You saw
that yourself. I'm totally helpless. Remember
the mess I made of your dinner?"

"Yeah, well it wasn't as bad as the mess *I've*
made of my dinner," Kate muttered.

So now I'm klutzy and *helpless,* she thought.
Great. Thanks for pointing it out, Allegra.

"I'm sure you'll feel better in a few days,"
Allegra pronounced. "You just need time to ad-
just. And then you'll feel great, and you'll look
much better. Back to your old self in no time."

Which means that I must look as bad as I feel,
Kate thought with a sigh. She squinted at Allegra
and then turned away, grunting.

Kate sat by the railing, focusing on the horizon as she'd been told, for most of the afternoon.
Justin and Allegra kept moving around the boat
together, smoothly and efficiently, as though
they'd been sailing together for years.

153

Kate couldn't help but notice how close they got to each other every time they had to switch positions. Or how tight and revealing Allegra's bathing suit really was.

The only thing even vaguely similar about the girl they'd met on the beach a few days ago and the woman who was on the boat with them now were the thick black glasses perched precariously on her nose.

Funny how with the ponytail and dowdy clothes the glasses had looked bookish and unflattering. But now, with her wild red hair and shapely body, the glasses somehow managed to look sexy. Kate watched as Allegra flashed Justin a perfectly white and captivating smile.

Damn her, Kate thought. *What is she doing? I think she's flirting with him. No—she's definitely flirting with him.*

"I really wish I could do *something* to help," Kate blurted out. "I'm beginning to feel like the fifth wheel here." She laughed unconvincingly.

Justin glanced at her and then just shook his head, as if to say, It's all your own fault, Kate. You wanted her along. You can't be mad at me if she doesn't get sick like you and throw up all over her shorts.

"That's all right," Allegra cried out sweetly and earnestly. "Justin is a great sailor. Don't worry about anything else. I'm taking care of it."

Right, Kate said to herself. *You sure are—and that's what's making me worry.*

"Come on, Justin, don't you think that she seems . . . different?" Kate pressed. They were at the back of the boat, where Kate knew it was safest to talk because the wind immediately whipped away all their words.

"What do you mean? Different how?"

"You know, when we met her she was . . . sort of clumsy . . . and sort of . . . gawky . . . and—"

"You mean she was a nerd," Justin stated.

"Well, no," Kate said quickly. "I mean, maybe a little. Not that I'm being *judgmental* or anything. But she did seem a little naive. That was the word *you* used, remember Justin?"

"Sure, I remember."

"But she was so, I don't know, harmless or something. I didn't think it would be any big deal asking her along."

"And now it's a big deal?" Justin asked.

"Just tell me honestly," Kate demanded, finally asking what she'd been curious about for the last two days. "Don't you see *anything* different about her. Anything *at all?*"

Justin glanced at Allegra, standing at the wheel, and looked quickly away. He shrugged. "Not really," he said, not meeting Kate's eyes.

Kate looked at Allegra herself and narrowed

her gaze. *Not really,* she thought. Now, that was a lie.

Allegra stood before them like a vision from the *Sports Illustrated* swimsuit issue.

Her hair flew out behind her, thick, curly, and wild. Her skin hadn't burned in the sun like some redheads', but instead had turned a creamy, orangey gold. Her long, slim legs looked even longer in her high-cut bathing suit, and her shoulders and arms were lean and muscled from steering and trimming the sail. Kate wondered wryly why Allegra was still sticking to one-pieces. She'd seen for herself the practically illegal bikinis Allegra owned. Just a token gesture of modesty, no doubt.

"Justin, you don't honestly expect me to believe that," Kate muttered.

"Believe what you want to believe, Kate. I don't know what you want me to say. Are you actually jealous of her?"

Kate blushed, realizing that she'd gone too far. "No," she said quickly. "I just wondered what you thought."

"No, you didn't," Justin said angrily. "You don't care what I think. You want me to say I find her attractive so you can be mad at me too."

"I *don't* want you to find her attractive," Kate cried, trying to keep her voice low.

"Well, don't push me, Kate," Justin exclaimed.

"I didn't want her here, did I? I wanted it to be you and me. I said that right from the beginning. So don't test me now."

Justin turned his head away, pretending to concentrate on the water behind them.

Kate was silent, burning with shame and hurt. Why had he spoken like that?

Allegra was getting more and more attractive. And Kate *was* jealous. And worried. She'd just wanted to know if anyone else, namely Justin, was noticing too.

Well, she had an answer to that, all right. Justin's reaction proved that Kate wasn't the only one who was noticing how Allegra was changing. Justin had eyes. He could see. But he was trying not to think about it. And he was lying to her by pretending otherwise.

Not surprisingly, she was starting to feel sick again.

"Kate," Justin said softly, turning back to her and drawing her into his arms, "I'm sorry I snapped at you. Forgive me?"

She tried a smile, though she couldn't quite give up the frown that dragged at the corners of her mouth.

"I know that you're not feeling so great," Justin said. "I can see that you're uncomfortable. But I'm also a little edgy, and that's because I can't do anything to make you feel better."

157

"I understand," Kate said sullenly.

"And to tell you the truth," he went on, "Allegra does look different. It happens when people take off their clothes and you see they have a figure. But remember, I spent lots of long summers looking at lots of bodies in lots of bikinis. A nice swimsuit isn't what I look for anymore, and it hurts to think that you think that about me."

"I'm sorry," Kate said quietly.

"And listen," Justin went on, "just so you can't misinterpret *this* too, I love you because you're *more* than just a beautiful body. But lucky me, you have that too—and a great swimsuit."

"Thanks, I think," Kate said.

"I'm also touchy about Allegra because I feel guilty about resenting her presence." Justin's breath was warm on Kate's neck. "And I do resent it," he said softly, "because I'm not alone with you—the way I wish I could be."

Kate sighed and leaned into him. It was good to be able to rest against him like this. Somehow his steadiness made her feel better—in her head *and* in her stomach.

The whole Allegra metamorphosis was just so eerie, Kate thought. Every time Kate looked at her, she couldn't help thinking she was really seeing someone else. She didn't know who, but definitely not the innocent girl they'd met on the beach.

TWELVE

Chelsea stood in the doorway to her parents' living room with baby Selena in her arms. Her eyes roamed around her childhood home. Everything was so familiar she could see it in her sleep: the mahogany dining-room table, the overstuffed sofas, the beautiful landscape of Chesapeake Bay that her father had commissioned and hung over the fireplace. And her raucous family in its usual confused uproar. Since the last time she was home, she'd gotten a new job and she'd gotten married. Oddly, though, nothing seemed different. Did Ocean City even exist?

"That baby looks good on you, hon," Chelsea's grandmother commented.

"Come on, now, give her time, give her time," Mrs. Lennox said. "She and Connor are just babies themselves. Give them time to settle into their lives together first."

"When I was Chelsea's age, I'd already had two little ones and another on the way," her grandmother said.

"Okay, Chels," Mr. Lennox boomed. "What is this news that you had us waiting to hear? Why is it that that boy—"

"Connor," Mrs. Lennox interjected, giving her husband a warning look.

"Why isn't *Connor* down here with you?" Mr. Lennox continued, repeating Connor's name distastefully.

Well, it *was* good news, Chelsea thought. She should be happy, even if the reality of what it was doing to her relationship with Connor wasn't as cool as the idea of it.

"An editor at a top publishing firm in New York wants to buy Connor's first novel," Chelsea said excitedly.

"Well, I'll be," B.D. said. "You mean that boy can actually *write*? I thought all that was a cover for the IRA or something."

"I have to confess," Chelsea's dad said, smiling, "I always wondered whether that boy would amount to anything."

"Daddy!" Chelsea complained.

"Now, I didn't mean anything by that," he said, stumbling over his excuse. "It's just that . . .

well . . . you two were married so young, you're not even fully formed yet. I was just, uh, *interested,* you might say, in the outcome of his, er, ambitions."

"Uh-huh," Chelsea said crossly, "Nice try, Daddy."

"Yeah, Dad," B.D. laughed. "I never saw you so tongue-tied."

"Well," Mr. Lennox said, his brow knitting with concentration. "We all knew that *you* definitely had great artistic talent, Chelsea. Let me just say that it's a pleasant surprise for Connor to be the first one to break out, so to speak. Maybe you should quit that job at the ad agency so you can keep up with his success."

Chelsea opened her mouth but nothing came out. She was speechless. It was as if her father had just pressed every one of her buttons, overloading her circuits. The result was paralysis.

Her mother put her arms around her. "When they get all that contract mess worked out," she said, obviously trying to change the subject, "maybe we can see about getting an excerpt printed in the magazine."

"*Your* magazine?" Marissa queried. "That magazine is by and for black people!"

"But he's my . . . well, son-in-law. We can make him an honorary member this one time, can't we?" she said, cracking the room up. "Besides,

161

it's my magazine. If I say it's in, it's in." She turned to Chelsea. "So when can I see a complete manuscript?"

"Well, that's the not-so-good-news part."

"Oh?" Mrs. Lennox said, raising her eyebrows.

"You see, they only saw three chapters. They asked to see the rest."

"So why doesn't he just stick it in the mail?" B.D. asked.

"He can't until he writes it," Chelsea blurted.

"Oh, I see," her mother said, obviously disappointed.

"So he hasn't *finished* anything yet," Mr. Lennox said, crossing his arms and putting on that I-was-right-the-first-time frown.

"That's why he's not here," Chelsea explained. "He's finishing his book as we speak. He hasn't slept or eaten in a week. He's doing nothing but writing. I haven't ever seen him so dedicated to anything."

"I *guess* that's a good reason for his not coming down," Marissa said, trying not to show her disappointment.

"Well, he's not here," B.D. said, "so there's no use crying about it."

"Well," Mrs. Lennox said, "they must have been promising chapters if they sparked that much interest. That's good enough for me. I suppose we can forgive him."

"What about you?" Chelsea asked Marissa. "Can you forgive him?"

"I can forgive anybody who's attached to you," Marissa said with a smile.

Suddenly there was commotion in the back of the room. Chelsea's grandmother was throwing her arms up in the air and covering her mouth, as if she were keeping herself from screaming at the top of her lungs.

"Mama?" Chelsea's mother asked, running to where her mother was sitting. "What is it, Mama?"

"Oh, I can't believe I could have done such a stupid thing," Chelsea's grandmother said. By this time everyone had gathered around her chair, thinking she was having a heart attack or something.

"Ooh, I'm a worthless old woman," she went on. "You should put me on an iceberg and send me off into the middle of the ocean like the Eskimos do."

Mr. Lennox stepped forward. "Did you leave the oven on, Rose?" he asked, suddenly concerned.

"No, worse than that."

"The coffee machine!" Mrs. Lennox blurted. "You left the—"

"No, no, nothing like that. I forgot—" She looked up at Marissa, laying a hand on her arm. "Honey, I forgot the *dress*."

"What dress?" Chelsea asked.

163

Marissa turned to her, obviously distraught. "Our family's ancestral christening dress."

"So we'll go out and buy you a new one," B.D. said. "That one is probably riddled with holes by now, anyway—"

"Bite your tongue, mister sailor," his grandmother snapped. "That dress was in perfect condition."

"It's not for *me,* B.D.," Marissa whined. "It's for Selena. It's the baby's dress."

"And every baby girl in this family for the last hundred and fifty years has worn that dress," their grandmother lectured. "Since the time this family were slaves in Georgia to today, when this family lives in this fine, fine house, that dress has brought every girl child into the world, including every woman standing in this room. It's our history. You can't turn your back on your history."

"But obviously you can forget it at home," B.D. murmured.

Chelsea gave her brother a swift kick on the ankle and eyed him mischievously. "Go ahead," she hissed.

"Go ahead what?" he hissed back.

"Offer."

"Offer what?"

"Offer to drive up to Pittsburgh tonight to get the dress," Chelsea whispered fiercely.

"Drive up to Pittsburgh tonight!" B.D. blurted out in full voice.

Their grandmother got to her feet and took B.D.'s face in her hands. "Oh, would you, B.D.? Would you really? You're such a good boy. You know how to make an old woman cry with joy," she said, dabbing her eyes with the sleeve of her dress.

"Thanks a lot," B.D. whispered to Chelsea with narrowed eyes. Then, plastering a smile on his face, he said, "No problem. Glad I can help."

Then his face lit up with a brilliant idea. Chelsea recognized that look. "But—but I wouldn't know what to look for once I got there," he said, eyeing Chelsea.

"I'll draw you a picture, B.D.," she said quickly. "Grandma will tell you exactly where it is, and I'll draw you a picture of what it looks like."

"I don't know," B.D. said, unable to hide his devilish grin. "I wouldn't want to drive all that way for nothing." He turned and looked straight at Chelsea. "I wouldn't want to mess up Selena's christening and undo all that *history*."

Chelsea kicked him again.

"Chelsea," B.D. asked innocently, "why are you kicking me? Are you offering to drive with me to Pittsburgh and rescue our family history?"

"All right, you two," Mrs. Lennox said. "That's

165

enough. It is a good idea for you to go with your brother, Chelsea. You can keep him company. And you can make sure he brings down the right dress, instead of one of my old nightgowns. Because we all *know* what taste he has in women's clothing!"

The room broke up in laughter.

"All right, all right," B.D. said. "We'll both go. But we should go now, so we can be back in time for that turkey you have in the oven, Mom."

B.D. craned his neck toward the back of the room. "Hey, Antonio, where are you? I almost forgot you were here, you were so quiet."

So did I, Chelsea thought, her heartbeat suddenly quickening.

"You ready for a ride, son?" B.D. asked.

"Anytime you're ready," Antonio replied.

"I didn't say *Antonio* had to go," Mrs. Lennox said demurely.

"Yeah," Marissa said, sidling up to Antonio's side. "Why don't you leave this good-looking soldier to protect the women back at the fort?"

"Come on, Antonio," B.D. said. "You come with Chelsea and me to keep us from killing each other before we get there. Anyway, I know you and Chels have a lot of catching up to do." He turned to the rest of the family and smiled. "You all can just go and protect your little own selves."

Suddenly his smile vanished, and his face twisted up with pain.

"Shoot!" B.D. exclaimed. "I completely forgot!" He looked meaningfully at Antonio. "Why didn't you remind me?"

"I forgot until just now, too," Antonio said.

"What did you forget, B.D.?" Chelsea asked. "And this better not be some dumb excuse to get out of this, because I'm not driving up there by myself."

"But you won't have to!" B.D. said excitedly, his face brightening.

"B.D., what's this all about?" Mr. Lennox boomed.

"Our captain is coming into town for a meeting at the Pentagon," B.D. explained. "Antonio and I are supposed to be his escorts for the afternoon. We offered to pick him up at the station, show him around a bit, then drop him off at his hotel."

"Well, he'll just have to find some other way to—" Chelsea began.

"Well, now, hang on a minute, Chelsea," Mr. Lennox said. "A man can't just break a promise to his captain. B.D. and Antonio would never hear the end of it."

"But I won't have to," B.D. said. "That's what I'm saying. I can pick up the captain. And Antonio can drive up to Pittsburgh with Chelsea."

"Oh, would you, young man?" Chelsea's grandmother asked, looking up at Antonio. "You'd be rescuing our family heritage."

"You could take my car," Mrs. Lennox said.

"Your car!" Chelsea said. "Your car is practically as old as I am."

"B.D. will need your father's to give his captain a tour, but mine should have enough life in it to get up to Pittsburgh and back."

"Well?" Antonio said, looking across the room at Chelsea. "What do you say, Chelsea? Are you willing to stay cooped up in a car for a few hours with an old friend?"

Chelsea felt Antonio's eyes bore into her like laser beams. The reaction was instantaneous: Her face flushed, her heart practically leaped out of her throat, her palms broke out in a sweat.

This is ridiculous, she thought. *I'm a married woman.*

But all she could do was smile.

"I take that as an affirmative," B.D. said, putting his arm around Chelsea.

Grace lay in bed with her eyes open, staring at the ceiling, marveling at her new realization. It was hard to believe, but true.

Sleeping in was just no fun anymore.

All it did was give her more time to dream

about David, or to think about how lonely she was now. And she'd spent almost the entire morning tossing and turning, wishing for blissful nothingness and instead being tormented by memories: The first time she'd met David, when she'd hijacked him to help Chelsea in the Best Body on the Beach contest. The look in his eye when she'd first admitted to him that she liked to park at the end of the airport runway to watch the planes take off. The two of them in the cockpit of his plane. On the porch of his bungalow. In his bed.

Grace winced. It was no use. Impossible but true, Grace had no desire to stay in bed now. She got up, pulled a long silk robe around herself, and began pacing the room, looking for something to do. The enormous bath in her private bathroom sat staring at her like a big marble eye. But sitting in it meant being relaxed, and Grace knew she couldn't lounge around in this mood.

She stalked onto the balcony, full of nervous energy, and began drumming her fingers on the railing and scanning the water intently as though any minute it would bring forth something miraculous and interesting. She needed something to do. Somewhere to go.

Face it, lady, she told herself. *You are Lonely with a capital L.*

She went back into her room, and her eyes

fell upon her bookcase. Newly ordered and alphabetized.

Reading. Now, there was a novel idea.

Grace absently ran her hand along the books. She remembered the way Wilton had talked about them, and looked at them, with such . . . reverence. It was wild, really, that someone could be so *obsessed* about something. It was almost as though he were in love. With books.

It was the reason she'd met him in the first place.

Admired my book, he did, Grace thought, chuckling to herself.

And it was the reason he'd taken the job she'd offered, so that he could sit around and read all day long.

There, now! That was something she could do. She could go check up on her newest employee. Make sure that he hadn't wandered away from his duties. Make sure that no pretty girls had come along and lured him away from his reading.

With something to do, Grace perked up. She put on a racy gold-colored bikini, wrapped a sheer scarf with a dazzling Moroccan print around her waist, grabbed her sandals and sunglasses, and headed down the stairs.

When she got to the beach, Grace wondered if someone had drowned. It looked as if there'd been an accident, or perhaps a spectacular rescue. But Grace didn't see any police cars or ambulances or Beach Patrol Jeeps. It wasn't the kind of crowd that gathered at disaster sights.

She walked closer and realized that although there were lots of bodies, they were all lying pretty much contentedly in the sun—even though they were packed as tightly as sardines. And they were all wearing bikinis.

Where are the men? Grace wondered. *A crowd of women doesn't usually gather without drawing a crowd of men.*

Unless there was one man that other mere mortals couldn't hope to compare to.

Grace could see now, as she walked slowly across the burning sand, that the crowd of female sunbathers was radiating from one central spot. The lifeguard stand was shimmering in the sun, and suddenly Grace knew exactly who was sitting there.

She paused about twenty yards away and leaned against one of the pilings of the boardwalk, shaking her head in amazement. She hadn't seen a reaction on the beach quite like that since Justin had first starting guarding all those summers ago.

"It just breaks your heart, doesn't it?" a voice to her left sighed.

Grace turned to find a gorgeous girl with sleek blue-black hair and green eyes beside her.

"Excuse me?" Grace asked.

"Him," the girl gestured to the lifeguard stand. "It hurts just to look at him. But it's the kind of hurt I don't mind."

Grace laughed.

"I know what you mean," she said before she could think about it. "I really need to start preparing myself better. I have to live with him."

Suddenly Grace knew what it must be like to be famous. There had always been women who were jealous of her for one reason or another. But she'd never seen a look of pure envy like the one she was seeing right now. The girl managed to retrieve her jaw from where it had dropped—somewhere near the domain of her exposed navel—and was just shy of drooling by a few drops of spit.

"You live with him?" the girl said in amazement. Grace nodded, and then wondered if the girl was going to pass out.

"May I ask you," the girl said carefully and respectfully, "where it is that you live?"

Grace hesitated a moment, thinking, *Do I really want to see this girl at my house every day for the rest of the summer?*

"I'm sorry," Grace answered. "I can't tell you that. To be honest," she explained kindly, "I really just can't bear the thought of a hundred girls holding midnight vigils in my backyard from now until September."

The girl sighed. "Well, can you at least tell me his name?"

"Carr," Grace answered. "Carr Savett. He's from Kansas."

"Wow," the girl said dreamily, walking toward the evergrowing crowd. "I drove through Kansas once."

"How wonderful for you," Grace said to the girl's retreating back.

She walked quickly past the crowd of women admiring Carr in his Beach Patrol shorts and made her way down to the beach stand that Wilton was in charge of.

Grace peeked slowly around the side of the stand. When she saw Wilton, she burst out laughing. She just couldn't help it. He really was a sight. His chair was pushed back against the stall into the only piece of shade. Even his toes were curled in out of the sun. He was leaning over an imitation-maple lap desk, which straddled his knees, an open book before him, furiously scribbling notes onto a pad of yellow legal paper.

Grace smiled and shook her head.

A pretty girl in a fluorescent string bikini approached and stood hesitantly before Wilton's chair. Grace saw Wilton stop writing and glance up just far enough, perhaps, to get a look at her knees.

"Can I help you, miss?" he asked finally, glancing up from his book, and back again, with lightning speed.

"Do you sell bandages?" the girl asked shyly.

"Why? Did you hurt yourself?" Wilton asked.

"Well," the girl said slowly, turning her back to him and looking over her shoulder at her heel, "I think I cut my foot on something."

Grace could hear Wilton sigh. *So much for the pretty-girl-after-some-sympathy ploy,* Grace thought.

"It doesn't look very bad to me," Wilton said after looking quickly down at her foot. "There's a clinic, you know, right on the boardwalk," he continued. "They'll have something. Or one of the lifeguards will have a kit."

"Oh, really?" the pretty girl asked, perking up.

"The nearest one is just down the beach about fifty yards," Grace offered, stepping out from the side of the little blue stand.

The girl leaned around Grace, trying to get a good look.

"Trust me," Grace added, "he's worth it."

The girl turned red and nodded. "Thanks," she muttered as she scurried away.

Grace heard a soft, low whistle and a chuckle

from behind her. She tossed back her hair and turned to say hello to Wilton, ready to confront another stare similar to the ones she'd gotten all along the beach. But when she turned around, she saw what he was chuckling and shaking his head over—he had underlined something in the pages of his book.

"This is great stuff," he mumbled.

Grace cleared her throat loudly.

"I know you're there, Grace." Wilton nodded. "Hello."

"Didn't your grandmother ever tell you that if you poked your nose in a book for too long, it would get stuck there?" Grace asked.

"Nope," Wilton replied, still reading and scribbling. "She said something like that about crossing my eyes, though."

"Oh, didn't I tell you? That'll happen too."

"It's a good book," Wilton responded, as though that should be enough.

Grace peered at the cover. *Absalom, Absalom!*, by William Faulkner.

"I'm sure it is," she said matter-of-factly. "But it's a good day too."

"Better book," Wilton said.

"Okay," Grace said tightly. "Try, I'm a good *boss*. And I've come to see that you're doing a good job."

Wilton paused for a minute, then went back

to his book. "Well, then," he finally said, "what do you think?"

"Excuse me?"

"Did I do a good job with the girl?" Wilton asked as he flipped a page and continued reading.

"Well, sure you did," Grace admitted.

"So everything's fine, right?"

But you didn't even look at her, Grace thought. *Not even once.*

"Sure," she answered automatically. "Everything's fine."

"Then you're happy, right?"

And you haven't looked at me either, Grace wanted to say. *I've turned every other head on this beach, thank you very much.*

"Because I really like this job," Wilton continued, nodding happily and pushing a stray piece of brown hair back out of his eyes. "I'm getting great reading done."

And just why are you suddenly so proud of turning heads? Grace demanded of herself. *You're in mourning, remember?*

"Glad to hear it," Grace replied stiffly.

"Thanks again, Grace," Wilton said. "And don't worry about the money and the receipts and stuff. That girl who lives with you came over and told me what to do."

"Who, Roan?" Grace asked.

"Yeah. She's one stand farther down from me, right? So now you don't have to come back tonight. I'll take care of everything myself."

"Great," Grace said, her voice flat.

She watched Wilton for another few minutes. He scratched his left calf with his right foot. He tapped his pencil on the lap desk a few times. He cackled once or twice. *I wonder what he thinks the juicy parts are,* Grace mused.

Finally Grace had to admit that it was clear he wasn't interested in having a conversation with her. *So much for getting out of the house,* she thought. *So much for having something to do.*

THIRTEEN

Kate dropped down to the starboard deck beside Allegra and braced herself against the rail. She lifted her face to the sun and pretended to smile so Allegra wouldn't notice how green she was. That was the beautiful thing about the sun in the middle of the ocean: It was so clear, and so pure, that seasick green could easily be mistaken for the bronze of a deep tan.

It could even be a new color, Kate thought to herself. All those ridiculously trendy names for different shades of green in those clothing catalogs: sage, celery, mist, jade, cassis, celadon, basil. And now, nausea.

Justin had taken the wheel in the stern. Everything was under control. It was just the opportunity Kate had been waiting for. A few minutes alone with Allegra.

She sighed and pretended to look content. The sea had calmed a little, the wind was steady and slow. She looked up at the sky and guessed it was well after noon. The eastern horizon was just beginning to redden with late-afternoon sunlight.

The wind fluttered in the sails and whispered through her hair. Other than that there was no noise. Complete silence. Complete peace.

Still, she couldn't get rid of this feeling of unease. Something about Allegra's transformation really dug at her. It was so gradual, one change at a time—first the hair, then the bathing suit, then the tan—it just seemed so calculated.

"Feeling better?" Allegra asked.

Kate smiled and nodded vaguely.

"Yeah, it's funny about being out on the water," Allegra said. "Someone who's seasick can actually look like they're sporting a pretty cool tan."

Kate frowned.

"Boy, Allegra, you weren't kidding about your sailing ability. You're really great on a boat."

"Thanks. I told you guys I was a different person out here."

You sure are, Kate thought to herself. *So different it makes me suspicious.* She looked at Allegra, smiling to cover up the fact that she was examining her face. What *was* it about her that was bugging Kate so much, besides how attractive she'd become?

I know, Kate thought. *It's her eyes. They're darting around all over the place, from the horizon, to Justin, to the back of the boat, to the sky, back to the horizon. It's as if she's looking for something, making mental notes, trying to figure something out. She's got some plans that she's not telling us.*

Kate had to know more. She was sure there was more to know. She had to get Allegra to talk.

"So you must be feeling pretty relieved," Kate prodded.

"What do you mean?" Allegra said.

"Back on open water. Out of the clutches of that guy."

"That guy," Allegra said a little uncertainly.

"Yeah. The one in Florida."

"Florida?"

"You know, the state?"

"Oh, *that* guy," Allegra said, laughing. "I'm sorry, Kate. It's just that it was so painful that I've tried to block most of it out."

"Oh, of course," Kate said, eyeing her suspiciously. "So where did you say you're from again?"

Allegra shot a glowering stare Kate's way, then covered it up with a sickly sweet smile. But not before Kate noticed.

"My, you're just overflowing with questions today," Allegra said tightly.

"It comes with the seasickness," Kate said with a laugh. "You tend to overflow with a whole variety of things."

"Well, let me see," Allegra said. "Where should I begin? You know, I've sort of lived all over. My father was in the army, and we went from base to base to base until I was seventeen. I forget how many homes I've had. I hardly remember any of them. It's just one big blur."

Well, that's convenient, Kate thought. "So, anyway, I bet you're pretty excited to be going to Ocean City," she said.

"I can't wait," Allegra replied excitedly. "I can't wait to eat fried clams on the boardwalk. At, um, what's it called? Ricky's Salad Shack?"

Kate raised her eyebrows. "Ricky's, that's right. But—"

"Right on the boardwalk between the pizza place and the ice-cream stand."

"Well, yes," Kate said, confused. "But you said you'd never been there before."

"Oh, did I?" Allegra said, laughing a little too loudly. "Right. Of course. It's just that my grandparents have told me so much about the place for so long, I can see it clearly in my mind, like I've been there a hundred times."

"Grandparents?" Kate inquired.

"Yeah, they're so sweet," Allegra said charmingly. "Little old people. They send me a crisp five-dollar bill every month to help out with the rent." She laughed. "Isn't that funny, Kate? As if five dollars is the difference between having a place to live and being out on the street."

Kate frowned at Allegra, then studied her closely.

"What's the matter, Kate?" Allegra asked, forcing her face into a plastic grin. "Did I say something wrong?"

"Grandparents? In Ocean City?"

"Yeah. My, uh, mother's parents. They live in a sweet little saltbox house right on the—"

"But you said it was your aunt and uncle," Kate said flatly.

Allegra looked at Kate like a frightened deer. Her mouth hung open for a moment, then closed.

Suddenly Justin called from the stern. "Allegra, I'm going to bring her about. Would you get over there and keep an eye on the boom?"

"Sure!" Allegra cried, hopping to her feet. "Duty calls!" she shouted to Kate.

She stripped off her T-shirt and started to bound across to the other side, then stopped and took off her glasses and left them on the deck beside Kate. "Here, keep an eye on these, okay?" she asked. "Just stay comfortable, and don't forget to keep your eyes on the horizon, just like Justy said!"

Justy? Kate thought, watching Allegra's

muscular legs pump against the boat's rocking to keep her level.

There it was. Finally. That incredibly sexy string bikini she had seen in Allegra's bag. Or, rather, there it wasn't. So little of her was hidden, it was hardly worth the effort. She was a total knockout.

Something's definitely wrong, Kate thought. *She's been to Ocean City before, that's obvious. No one would know about Rick's hole-in-the-wall Clam Bar unless they'd been there.*

She and Allegra traded fake smiles across the boat.

And why'd she lie about her aunt and uncle?

Kate picked up Allegra's glasses and began fumbling with them, watching her and Justin banter back and forth about boat stuff. Justin wasn't even looking at her. He was looking at everything *but* her, as if he were *afraid* to. And who could blame him? Her glasses had been the final touch. They were the only thing keeping her from looking incredibly gorgeous. But now they were gone too. And now she *did* look incredibly gorgeous.

Allegra was making no attempt to hide her own admiring gaze for Justin. She studied his muscular chest, broad, tanned shoulders, and handsome, chiseled face, then smiled over at Kate. Kate seethed. It was as if Allegra were seducing him right in front of her.

But that's strange, Kate suddenly thought, toying with Allegra's glasses again. How could Allegra see that far without them? They were so thick. She'd said she was practically blind without them.

Kate put them to her face and looked through. Her jaw dropped. She turned to look through the frames out at the water, then at various things on the boat, including Allegra. They made no difference. Nothing was fuzzy or out of focus. They weren't prescription glasses at all. They were just plain glass! Phony!

Just like Allegra.

"Hey, what's that?" Justin cried, pointing off the starboard side.

"What?" Kate said, pulling herself up by the rail.

Allegra had hopped back to the stern and stood beside Justin. From where Kate stood, or rather hunched and wobbled, Allegra seemed to be doing more than just standing beside him. She seemed to be sidling up to him. Their knees were touching, their hips were grazing. If anybody saw them now, they'd think they were a couple for sure.

Justin reached underneath the controls and pulled out his telescope. Kate strained her eyes but didn't see anything. Then she did. A white glimmer on the horizon.

"What is it?" she asked.

"It's a sail," Justin said. "It's about the size of a yacht sail, not much bigger than us."

"So what?" Kate cried back to him.

"It's just that—I don't know," Justin said, lowering the telescope. "It's just that it seems to be on the same course as us. Like it's following us."

Kate squinted. "Could it be a coincidence?"

"Two boats heading in the exact same direction in open water? Sure, I guess so. But a pretty big one," Justin answered.

"Can I have a look?" Allegra asked, motioning for the telescope.

"Here you go," Justin said, handing it to her.

Allegra leveled the telescope, then seemed to double-clutch it, leaning forward.

Kate could see her mouth tighten into a straight line. Then she bit her lip.

"See anything interesting?" Kate called out to her.

Allegra lowered the telescope. "Nope," she said, handing it back to Justin. "Just another boat on the ocean." Her voice was carefully impassive, but Kate wasn't buying it. She could tell Allegra was upset.

Kate stepped over to the stern, clutching at the railing all the way. As she got closer, Justin sort of sidestepped away from Allegra.

Allegra's eyes narrowed at her.

185

"Here," Kate said, taking Allegra's glasses out of her pocket. "Don't you need these?"

The two girls stared at each other while Justin just looked confused. Then Allegra broke into a smile.

"You were doing pretty well without them," Kate said with a sneer.

"Thanks," Allegra said uncomfortably, taking the glasses and putting them on. "It's a low prescription. It's weird. Some things are as clear as day. And other things seem hidden behind a bank of clouds."

"Really," Kate quipped. "That's a new one. On-again-off-again shortsightedness. Never heard of that before." She shook her head. "Boy, the things they come up with nowadays."

Allegra smiled tightly and walked off.

Kate had tipped her hand, just as she'd intended. Allegra knew that she knew something now. But what did Kate really know? She knew what Allegra *wasn't*. But she had no idea what Allegra really *was*.

FOURTEEN

Familiar scenery was whipping by as Chelsea and Antonio drove north through Washington. Places she used to shop, meet with her friends, play in her softball league. Places she'd gone to with Antonio, taking buses through the surrounding towns hand in hand, conquering the land like two little explorers. They'd been good friends. Too young to kiss. Too young to think they had to.

They didn't speak much, at first. There seemed too much to say. *Where do we start talking? Chelsea wondered. Where does a lifelong friendship start again after a two-year intermission?*

"So where is your father stationed now?" Chelsea asked, making small talk as she banked onto the interstate that would take them to Pittsburgh.

"He's a drill sergeant in Texas," Antonio said. "It's been tough for him without my mom."

"Miss her?" Chelsea asked.

"Miss her?" Antonio repeated. "I think about my mother every day. I feel her with me all the time. I can feel her with us right now. Sitting in that backseat, backseat driving like she always did with me and my dad. 'Antonio, you're driving too fast! Antonio, you're driving too slow!'"

They broke up in laughter. "Yeah, I remember nothing was ever perfect enough for your mom," Chelsea said.

"Perfection was in her blood, all right," Antonio said.

"And yours," Chelsea said meaningfully.

A long, awkward silence followed.

Why'd I say that? Chelsea chided herself. *Why do I keep complimenting him? Am I just trying to butter him up, or am I trying to convince myself that he's as good as I always thought?*

"Hey!" Antonio said, suddenly coming to life and turning toward Chelsea. "Remember that time I sneaked you out of your house and we went to the school yard and shot baskets and swung on the swings until dawn?"

Chelsea nodded. "How could I forget? Boy, we were something, weren't we? We were inseparable."

Antonio stared ahead at the road. "Then you started growing," he said. "And before I knew it, you were this beautiful young thing. It was that one summer. In June you were a girl. By September you'd turned into this . . . this—"

"Yes?" Chelsea egged him on.

Antonio was blushing. "Well, everybody started looking at you. I couldn't be around you so much anymore."

"I remember that," Chelsea murmured. "One day you were there. And it seemed the next you were gone. Completely out of my life."

"It wasn't as though I had anything better to do, Chelsea," Antonio tried to explain. "It was just that I couldn't stand to be around you if I wasn't your . . . well, you know."

"No," Chelsea said, smiling, "I *don't* know."

Antonio, obviously working up courage, took a deep breath. "If I wasn't your boyfriend," he said.

"I would have said yes in a second," Chelsea said, feeling half-sad because she had missed the opportunity, and half-safe, because she knew she couldn't now.

Antonio tapped his knee, deep in thought.

"So say it now," he finally said.

"Say what now?"

"Say yes."

Chelsea shot a worried look across the seat.

"Just for the heck of it," Antonio added quickly. "For old time's sake. It's too late now, anyway—"

That's right, she thought. *It's too late now.*

Chelsea smacked her lips. "Yes," she said. Then she blinked. And suddenly she had a vision. The man next to her was not a long-lost friend, but her husband. And Connor Riordan had never existed. She was Chelsea Palmer. And two little Palmers, Caleb and Noah—her two favorite boy's names—were raising hell in the backseat. And she was an artist, making money, illustrating the various marine bases they'd be moving in and out of as her Antonio worked his way up in the corps. And he called her "dear" and "honey" and "baby." And she called him "my Antonio."

My Antonio. My Antonio . . . it had a poetic ring to it.

Chelsea blinked again and the vision was gone. The white lines on the highway ran on endlessly, converging in a spot far away. The man sitting in the passenger seat to her right wasn't her husband. He was just an old friend. A lost chance. A case of bad timing.

"I have to confess something," Antonio said shyly. "I promised myself I would never tell you. But I feel like I can say it now and you'll take it the right way."

Chelsea tightened her grip on the wheel. She knew what was coming. Unconsciously, deep inside her, she'd been expecting it.

"When you were married—"

"Yes," Chelsea said.

"When you married—"

"Connor."

"Connor. When I heard you'd married Connor, I didn't speak to anybody for a whole week. I didn't open my mouth. I didn't have anything to say. I couldn't even write you and say congratulations."

Chelsea nodded with understanding.

"I was upset," Antonio said.

This was getting too heavy. Chelsea tapped Antonio playfully on the knee and winked. Though inside she wasn't laughing.

"Now, come on," she snickered. "You can't tell me a good-looking marine like you can't get a date every night."

Antonio didn't even crack a smile. "I don't know," he said dreamily, staring out the side window. "I don't date much. I guess I'd always hoped that after I got out of the academy—"

"Hey, now, would you look at that?" Chelsea cut in, pointing out the window at a convoy of army trucks passing the other way, toward Washington. "Looks like someone is invading our capital!" she said.

191

She smiled sadly at Antonio. She was glad she'd stopped him from saying what he was about to say. Talking like this wouldn't do either of them any good. What was done was done. The past was past.

"May as well catch some shut-eye," Antonio said, tipping his midshipman's cap over his face. "Looks like it's going to be a long afternoon."

Marta wheeled up to the outdoor table grinning like a Cheshire cat. Grace had known when they'd made this lunch date that Marta would be eager to see her. Grace smiled and shook her head, knowing exactly what Marta's first question was going to be.

"Soooo?" Marta asked eagerly, drawing the word out as she scooted her chair into place.

"What?" Grace asked innocently.

"Come on," Marta cried, grabbing her straw and flicking water across the table at Grace. "How *is* he? Don't keep me in suspense. You know I picked him especially for you, Grace. So tell me what you think."

"Carr?" Grace shrugged noncommittally. "He's a nice guy. Sure. And he's nice looking—"

"Nice looking?" Marta's jaw dropped. "You *did* see the public-health hazard he caused on the beach yesterday?"

"People have drawn crowds before," Grace argued. "Justin used to get that kind of attention."

"Yeah, well, Justin isn't here. And he already has a girlfriend," Marta pointed out.

"Never a truer word," Grace replied. "And so does Carr."

"Carr?" Marta squeaked. "He has a girlfriend? Already? You're kidding!"

"Not a local," Grace explained. "He's a good boy, you know. He's got a girl *back home*."

"Well, back home is pretty far away, right?" Marta asked.

"Yeah." Grace smiled. "All the way back in Kansas. But her picture's hanging right above his bed. I'll bet he even kisses it good night."

Marta paused just long enough to give the waitress her order before she got back to her cross-examination.

"And they talk regularly?" Marta pressed.

"I think so. Pretty regularly," Grace replied. "I picked up a call from her the other day," Grace admitted, her eyes sparkling with mischief. "I do wonder what our little boy told her, because she sure seemed surprised to hear my voice."

"And?"

"She sounded like an unholy bitch is all," Grace remarked wryly. "She probably had a pitchfork in her hand. I swear I heard her

193

knuckles crack through the phone as she gripped it. She wants to kill me."

"I can't blame her," Marta muttered.

"Why? I'm not interested," Grace insisted.

Marta raised her eyebrow.

"Maybe there's superficial attraction," Grace admitted. "I'm not *blind.* But that doesn't mean I'm *interested.*"

"Of course not," Marta replied. "You're still heartbroken over David."

"I am!" Grace cried, suddenly angry.

Marta put her hand out and touched Grace on the shoulder. "I know," she said soothingly. "I wasn't being mean. I know you're hurt, because David was—is—a great guy. It's just that soon enough you'll realize that you need to move on. You can't swear off men completely," Marta said softly.

"I know that," Grace answered, "but I'm just not ready yet. I don't know when I will be. All those memories are so fresh, you know? I realize there are men around—handsome, interesting, no doubt. But I just don't know. And Carr? He may be too much right now, even for me."

Marta nodded and leaned back as the waitress brought over their sandwiches.

"And then, of course, there's Wilton," Grace continued, spearing a french fry with her fork before her plate hit the table. "You met him."

"No, actually, I didn't," Marta laughed. "Remember, you told him not to bother!"

"Oh, right." Grace chuckled. "Well, I didn't mean for him to take me literally."

"He does look like a very—how shall I say it?—*literal* guy," Marta noted.

"Literal and literary," Grace said. "Only one way of looking at the world, and one obsession. That's two dangerous characteristics, if you ask me."

"You sound put out, Grace," Marta said, peering closely at her friend. "Are you bothered that he doesn't have . . . *outside* interests?"

"Of course not!" Grace cried. "Did I tell you that he spent the entire night of your going-away party organizing my bookshelf?"

"Well, that's kind of cute, actually," Marta said. "It might not be so bad to go on a date with him, or with Carr. At the very least it could be fun, or funny."

"No way," Grace said, brushing the thought aside with her hand. "I'm not ready yet, and besides . . . Carr already has a girlfriend he's very loyal to. And Wilton . . ." Grace struggled for a minute. "I mean, Wilton?" She shook her head. "He's an employee," she finally said.

"Not that you've given it any thought at all," Marta said, sipping on her iced tea. "Grace, sorry, but you're incapable of forgetting about guys."

"Not incapable," Grace exclaimed. "That's a little strong, don't you think?"

"What I think is that within a week you'll be scheming about ways to go after Carr, Wilton, or both at once," Marta cried.

"Both at once!"

"A bet," Marta suggested. "Ten bucks."

Grace tilted her head back and stared down the length of her nose. "You're on."

Chelsea got out of the car and stood staring up at her grandmother's house. It was an old Victorian, with teardrop brocade hanging off the roof and a huge wraparound porch.

"Wow, does this house bring back memories," she said. "There's that swing-seat. I used to sit on that and swing all day—swing myself to sleep."

She and Antonio took the steps to the porch slowly. At the top Chelsea made for the swing and sat down. She patted the conspicuously empty space beside her.

At first Antonio didn't move.

"Come on," she said. "I won't bite."

"It's not you I'm afraid of," he said.

"I'm a big girl," she said, smiling broadly. "I can control myself."

Antonio sat beside her.

"Look what's happened to this neighborhood," Chelsea said, looking up and down the street. Some of the houses, some as big and beautiful as this one, were boarded up. Broken glass covered the sidewalks like a carpet of pebbles. Litter was everywhere.

"This used to be one of Pittsburgh's most exclusive neighborhoods," she said wistfully. "My grandmother says that people used to take pride in it, sitting on their stoops in the evening, calling to each other across the road. Kids used to play in these streets. Now they just sell drugs in the alleyways between houses."

Antonio's hand came to rest on top of Chelsea's, but she pretended not to notice.

"Why doesn't she move out?" Antonio asked.

"That's a good question," Chelsea said. "It's not like we don't have enough money to buy her a new house or anything. Or even have her come down and live with us. But she's stubborn as a mule. She says she was born here, and she's going to die here. It's what she knows."

Antonio kicked at the floor, and the swing started to move back and forth, slowly, slowly.

Chelsea closed her eyes. "It's like I'm a little girl again," she said. Then her eyes popped open, and she stared straight into Antonio's. She felt an uncontrollable urge just to lean over and . . .

"Come on, sailor!" she said, leaping to her feet. "We're here on a mission. Let's do it!" She handed Antonio the key ring. "See what you can do with this key."

Antonio took the house key and stepped toward Chelsea. He wasn't smiling anymore. He aimed the key at her heart and pressed it against her, as if he were trying to unlock something.

"Is this the key to your heart, Chelsea?" he asked.

"I don't know," she whispered shakily. "Two years ago it might have been."

Grace stepped through the door, breathed a sigh of relief at the end of another day, and began to brush the sand out of her hair, when the phone rang. She stared at it.

"Let the machine answer it," she said. "I'm too tired to talk."

But the phone stopped ringing and the machine didn't do a thing.

"I *hate* when people hang up and don't leave a message," she said.

Then she heard heavy footsteps coming up the stairs.

"Grace? Grace, are you home?" Carr called.

"Oh, hi, Carr," Grace said.

Carr held out the portable phone. "It's some guy named Wilton on the phone. He says it's important. Are you home?"

Grace didn't answer at first. She was too distracted by the way Carr filled the room. She took off her beach robe and dropped it onto the couch, taking delight in the deep shades of red Carr's face took on at the sight of her in her bikini. For some reason she just loved to do that to him.

"Sure, I guess," she finally said, holding out her hand.

As Carr came closer, his eyes drilled into her forehead, not daring to look any lower.

"Hello?" Grace said, chuckling to herself as Carr went into the kitchen.

"Grace, we have a real problem here," Wilton said urgently.

Grace plopped down onto the couch. "What is it, Wilton?"

"Well, toward the end of the day—you know how it is, you're hot, you're tired—"

"You've been reading all day," Grace quipped. "Yeah, yeah, go on. So what happened? You lost your bookmark?"

Wilton was silent. She could hear his frustration through the phone wires.

"Sorry," she said, "I forgot. Sarcasm detection at work. Just joking, Wilton. I'm listening."

"So I was a little distracted and I forgot—I'm really embarrassed to admit this, Grace."

"What happened, Wilton?" Grace asked, suddenly alarmed.

"I forgot to make the cash deposit," Wilton blurted.

"But you have the cash, right?" Grace asked quickly.

"Well, yeah," Wilton said, as though what else would he have done with it? "Of course."

Grace relaxed and breathed a sigh of relief. She watched Carr crisscrossing the kitchen as he made himself a sandwich. "So no big deal," she said. "Just deposit the receipts in the bank tomorrow with tomorrow's. Okay? Anything else?"

"Well, yeah," Wilton said sheepishly. "It's all that cash."

"All that cash what, Wilton?" Grace asked a little impatiently. All she wanted was a shower and to have a big cold glass of orange juice.

"It's sitting here right in front of me."

"Good," Grace said. "That's a good place for it. Keep your eye on it until tomorrow."

"You trust me?" Wilton asked, surprised.

"Of course I trust you," Grace said. "That's why I hired you."

"But, but—I don't know if *I* trust me," Wilton said.

Grace laughed. "Don't think about it, Wilton. I'm sure your parents won't steal any! If you go out and buy a book, just make sure I get to read it after you."

"Look, let me just bring the money over, Grace,

please? I have this thing about having a lot of money. I don't like it around. It attracts attention and makes me nervous."

"Close the window shades," Grace said sternly. "And don't answer the door. Then no one will know it's there."

"Please, Grace? Let me just bring it over. I can be there in ten minutes."

"Wait," Grace said. She made a quick survey of the house. Roan and Bo were nowhere to be seen. Just Carr, looking perfect as always. But otherwise, a totally empty house.

"All right, Wilton. But I'll tell you what," Grace said. "I'll come over there. Stay put."

"Oh, that's excellent, Grace," Wilton said. "Excellent. Thanks a lot."

"Keep your eye on that money, now, Wilton," Grace ordered.

"No problem," Wilton said.

Just as Grace turned off the phone, it rang again.

"Wait!" Carr said, bounding in from the kitchen. "That's Jody."

Grace looked quizzically at the phone. "How do you know?"

Carr's face sagged with a sort of beaten look. "I don't know," he said unhappily. "I can just tell."

"Well, here you go," Grace said, happily handing over the phone. "Wouldn't want to get between you and your ESP."

Grace waited as Carr answered, "Hello?"

As his expression went from hopeful expectation to disappointment to frustration to total defeat, she knew he was right. It was Jody. And she was unloading her daily shipment of grief.

"B-but, Jody . . . b-but, baby . . . no, nothing like that . . ." Carr was stuttering.

She shook her head. It was painful to listen to. Why was this gorgeous guy keeping up a long-distance relationship with the Wicked Witch of the West?

Grace gathered her beach robe, her keys, her wallet.

What else? she wondered, looking around the house. Nothing, really, but why wasn't she just leaving?

But why should *I?* she realized. Why willingly leave the presence of such a perfect specimen of manhood like Carr?

But leave she must.

As she was turning to go, she spied a pen on the coffee table in front of the love seat Carr had dropped into.

You never know when you'll need a pen, she said to herself.

Then, on impulse, rather than merely walk around the love seat and pick up the pen, Grace

202

leaned over Carr's shoulder, making sure to give him her full weight, and stretched for the pen. Of course her beach robe was going to fall open in front of his face. Of course she happened to have on one of her most provocative bikinis. She could feel his scratchy five-o'clock shadow against her skin. It sent shivers of possibility up her spine.

Suddenly Carr began to cough into the phone. Grace could see his neck heat up with embarrassment. She smiled, gratified by the catch in his voice.

"No, no, baby, there's no one here. Grace just left . . . Lying? Why would I lie?"

But as Grace stepped outside, listening to Carr's pathetic pleas through the door, she suddenly became annoyed.

"Way to go, Grace," she chided herself. "And how old are we? Fifteen? I thought you outgrew those games years ago."

And poor Carr. He's obviously catching hell. Poor guy. "He deserves better," she said aloud. "He definitely deserves better."

"Would you look at this!" Chelsea cried, digging into a trunk up to her elbows. "Look at all this stuff."

They had found the dress immediately, wrapped neatly in cloth exactly where Chelsea's grandmother had said it would be. But that had been an hour ago. Since then Chelsea had been bounding from chest to chest, trunk to trunk, sifting through 150 years of family history.

And Antonio had sat down on a box and waited patiently. His eyes followed her everywhere. Chelsea could feel them on her.

"Look at these photographs," she cried. "These must be a hundred years old!"

Chelsea brought the old album over to Antonio and leaned against his leg as they leafed through it. Families in formal attire, black suits, petticoats. The women were seated and the men were propped behind them. Barns and tractors and farm implements stood in the background.

"Where are they?" Antonio asked.

"Georgia, I guess," Chelsea said. "But this could be anywhere. After the Civil War, the family spread out. Some stayed to work the farm. Some came up here, to Pittsburgh. Some went to Chicago, some New York."

Antonio peered at the photograph. "It doesn't much look like New York," he said.

"But don't they look serious? They always look so somber in these old pictures," Chelsea said.

"It's just the way they wanted to be remembered," Antonio remarked. "As serious, hard-working folks. And besides, they had reason to be somber. They wanted to leave the South, but they weren't really welcome in the North. We're lucky that we were born when we were, with all of that way behind us."

"Boy, it sure makes you feel *connected,* though, doesn't it?"

"What do you mean?"

"To family. You know, to your past, your history. It makes me feel more . . . I don't know—"

"Black?" Antonio asked.

"I guess that's it. I don't know," Chelsea said.

"What about Connor?" Antonio asked.

"Connor?" The name startled her. It was almost as if he hadn't existed for the last few hours. It was almost as if she wasn't married. "What *about* Connor?" she asked.

"I didn't mean anything, Chelsea," Antonio said quickly. "I just mean about . . . you know . . . the stuff we're talking about. Your history. Your legacy."

"You mean because Connor is white?" Chelsea asked.

Antonio shrugged.

Chelsea looked away. She felt a pang of guilt. She'd thought she'd dealt with all that. All that mixed-marriage stuff. But here it was again. Would it keep coming back to haunt her?

"Oh my god!" she cried, making an obvious

205

effort to change the subject. She lifted a bundle of old letters. "I can't believe she saved these. These were old letters and valentines and stuff from when I was *really* young."

Chelsea began leafing through them. She stopped to study one, a beautiful lacy valentine card, and held it up to the dim light. She frowned.

"Nineteen eighty-six," she said. "I was twelve. I never did figure out who sent me this one. I got one from everyone in the class, and they were all signed except this one. But this one was the prettiest."

Antonio cleared his throat and smiled. "That was mine," he said.

"Yours? But . . . Antonio, why didn't you sign your name? It wasn't any secret that we were friends. We spent almost every day together."

"It's what I was trying to tell you back there in the car, Chelsea. We *were* friends. But I always wanted more. I just couldn't admit it."

"Even then?" Chelsea said, her voice laced with disbelief.

"Even then," Antonio said simply.

Chelsea suddenly realized how close they were. She was leaning on his leg. She could feel his strong thigh muscles beneath his uniform. She could smell him. A subtle waft of woodsy cologne. She could practically feel his breath on her face when he talked.

Antonio leaned toward her. She didn't move. She couldn't.

He leaned past her and picked up something off the pile of old letters and pictures. It was an old brass skeleton key, long and heavy, with delicately cut teeth.

He held it up to her. It glinted in the light.

"What's this, Chelsea?"

"An old family heirloom. Grandma used to bring it down every once in a while and tell us the story about it. It's the key to the cabin our family lived in on the Georgia plantation. When they left for the north, they took it with them. And since then every mother has put in her will that this key will be handed down to the oldest girl."

"Why only the girls?" Antonio asked.

"I guess because girls, and women, remember more," Chelsea said.

Antonio gently pressed the key against Chelsea's heart. "What about this key, Chelsea? Is this the one?"

FIFTEEN

Justin's eyes opened automatically. He sat up and looked into the darkness of his and Kate's belowdecks bedroom. Something was strange in the way the boat was moving. Something wasn't right.

He shook Kate awake.

"Kate?"

Kate groaned.

"Kate, get up," he commanded. She popped up beside him, immediately wide awake.

"What is it?"

"Listen," Justin said. "You feel anything funny?"

"I feel the boat moving. And I feel dinner moving in my stomach. And I feel like I'm going to throw up. But what else is new?"

"The way the boat's running is new," Justin said. "The wind's been on our starboard quarter since we left. But now we're running straight with it."

"Are you sure?" Kate asked.

"I know this boat better than I know myself. I'd know the way it would feel if it was painted purple. And I know we're running with the wind. Get up. We've changed course. Something happened. I know it."

Justin hopped up and started putting on his shorts.

"But Allegra's on night watch," Kate said. "She can steer, can't she?"

"She can steer, all right," Justin said, throwing open the hatch.

I knew it, Kate thought to herself. *I should have said something to Justin about her. There's something bad about her. I feel it in my bones.*

Outside, the moon hung high and brilliant in the sky, like a peephole to another universe. The light played in the waves, drawing a straight white road to the horizon.

The second he got on deck, Justin knew he'd been right. Allegra had crowded on sail and was making due east.

"Allegra!" he called.

She didn't answer.

Justin made for the stern and stopped in his tracks. Allegra was leaning back against the wind, her lush auburn hair flowing before her like a giant hood. What was she wearing? It wasn't much. A white thong, a white bikini top that showed more than it concealed. How could this be the same girl who'd dropped their dinner in the restaurant? She was stunning. He'd seen thousands of beautiful women when he was lifeguarding on the beach; but Allegra wasn't only one of the most beautiful he'd ever seen, she had an alluring quality. Magnetic. Something about her sucked you in—and made you forget everything else.

Except this boat. Justin shook himself out of his reverie and stepped forward. He was captain of the *Kate* first, and a guy second.

"What's going on?" he barked.

Allegra turned her beautiful face toward him. She smiled demurely, then stepped from behind the wheel, giving him a full view of her near-naked body.

Then she quickly hopped back and frowned. Justin felt Kate move up behind him.

"Allegra, would you mind explaining all this?" Justin said.

"Explaining what?" she asked innocently.

"The position of the moon, for one," Justin said.

Allegra raised her face. The moonlight made her skin look translucent. "Isn't it beautiful? You can almost feel it on your skin, like the sun."

"But it's in the wrong place," Justin said.

Allegra laughed. "Don't be silly," she said.

"Either the moon is in the wrong place, or we are," Justin said sternly.

"Justin, I don't know what you're talking about," Allegra said.

"Then why are we crowded on sail?"

"Crowded on sail?" she asked, as if she'd never heard the term.

"I'm not fooling around, Allegra!" Justin said, his voice rising with anger. "Why did we change course? Why are we heading east? When we went to bed, we were headed north-northwest. Have you read the compass lately?"

A worried look crossed Allegra's face. "Oops," she said. "I forgot. I don't know. I don't remember looking at it. Maybe I misread it."

"Misread a compass!" Justin cried. "A ten-year-old can read a compass!"

At that moment Allegra's eyes grew wide with fear. "Oh, my God," she shrieked.

Justin and Kate whirled around to see what she was looking at. "Oh, my God," Kate echoed.

Barely visible in the darkness before them loomed the glowing sand of a white beach. They were going to crash.

Grace knocked on the door of Wilton's condo. A moment later the door swung open, and there stood Wilton, smiling stupidly.

"Hi, there," he said, stepping aside so Grace could enter. She wrapped her beach robe more tightly around her and looked around the room. Pretty normal. Couch, TV, chairs, coffee table. What was she expecting? She didn't know. Maybe shelves and shelves of books, or piles of literary journals.

Wilton stood in the middle of the floor, clasping and unclasping his hands.

"So," he began uncomfortably.

"So," Grace countered.

"A drink?" Wilton offered, waving toward his parents' bar cart against the wall.

"OJ?" she asked.

"Sure," Wilton said. "But you sure you won't join me in a real drink? I mean, my parents aren't home or anything."

"Thanks, Will—Wilton," Grace said, smiling tightly. "Juice is fine."

"I think I'll have a beer myself."

"It's your house," Grace said, dropping into the couch.

When Wilton came back with the beer and the juice, he sat across the coffee table from Grace and crossed his legs.

"So," he started again.

"The money?" Grace asked. "Under the floorboards, maybe? Or behind the painting?"

"Under my bed," Wilton said nonchalantly.

212

"Who'd ever think to look there?" she said earnestly.

Wilton nodded. "I agree. Too obvious."

"Too obvious," Grace concurred, nodding. "So how do you like your job?"

"Excellent," Wilton said. "Halfway through *The Brothers Karamazov* already."

Grace nodded with appreciation. "Heavy stuff. I take it you've finished the Faulkner already. You're some quick reader. I'm saving that one for a rainy day. Or, rather, a rainy month. Or two."

"Really? You like Dostoevsky?"

"I liked *Crime and Punishment*. It made me sweat for weeks. It made me think I was guilty of some crime I never committed."

"I know what you mean," Wilton said, laughing gleefully. "I felt the same way. Boy, Grace, I can't tell you how great it is to talk to someone. I mean, really *talk* to someone."

"Thanks, Wilton. That's nice of you to say. So do you actually sell anything while I'm paying you to read?"

"Some," Wilton said. "I did almost two hundred dollars today."

"Two hun—" Grace exclaimed, moving to the edge of her seat. "Wilton, that's fantastic! That's a record."

Wilton just shrugged. "Girls love it when they think you're playing hard to get," he said.

"They'll buy stuff all day to get your attention."

Grace laughed a deep belly laugh and clapped her hands. She smiled at Wilton with genuine affection. "You're really something," she said, shaking her head.

Wilton tipped back his bottle of beer and let the last drop fall onto his tongue. He rose and headed for the kitchen. "You sure I can't get you a beer or something, Grace?" he asked.

"I didn't know you were such a drinker," Grace said.

"I'm not, really," Wilton said. "It's just that at the end of the day I like to . . . you know. It's just an end-of-the-day thing."

Suddenly he appeared before her, looking anxious. "You're not worried about me like that or anything, are you? Because if you are, you don't have to be. I mean, there's no problem at all. But if it makes you uncomfortable, I'll stop—"

Grace smiled and nodded. "Thank you for asking, Wilton. No. Your life is your life. As long as it doesn't affect your job, you do what you want. Deal?"

"Deal," Wilton said, sitting down with a glass of thick amber liquid.

Whiskey, Grace thought. She could smell it from across the room. A hazy cloud of ugly memories swept over her.

"I'll tell you something, Wilton," Grace said,

closing the distance between them with her concentrated gaze. "I don't know *why* I'm telling you this, exactly—I mean, I hardly know you. But if you keep working for me—and I hope you do— you'll probably find out sooner or later anyway."

"Yes?" Wilton asked. He leaned forward over his crossed knees. His eyes were clouded with concern.

This is definitely a guy I can be honest with, Grace told herself. *And comfortable with.*

"Drinking is a problem for me," Grace said.

"Oh," Wilton said, and immediately put his glass down on the coffee table.

"No," Grace said, laughing. "Not your problem. It's my problem. What I'm trying to say is that I'm an alcoholic. I mean, I was. Well, I guess you always are one. Forever. But what I mean to say is that I'm not drinking anymore. I can't. It'll ruin my life. I almost ruined my life once. I won't make that mistake again."

Wilton nodded and stayed silent. He waited for Grace to go on. But that was enough for now.

"That's all," Grace said. "No biggie, right?"

"Right," Wilton said. "Absolutely."

They sat in silence for a minute.

"Uh, Grace?" Wilton asked.

"Do you mind that I told you?" Grace asked worriedly. "Maybe you didn't want to know. I'm sorry—"

"No, no. I'm glad you told me. I mean, I appreciate your honesty. But I also appreciate the fact that you trusted me. Thank you."

Grace smiled. "No, Wilton, thank *you*."

Suddenly Wilton looked up at the clock on the wall. "Oh, my God," he cried. "Oh, my God."

Grace shot up out of her chair. "What? What is it?"

"I'm missing *F Troop!*"

"You're missing what?"

"*F Troop*. It's my favorite TV program. Reruns at seven every day."

"That's a good one, Wilton. For a second there—"

"No, I'm serious Grace. You sit here," he said, waving her over to his chair. "And I'll sit over here." He pulled another chair next to Grace's. "Come on, we're missing it!"

Grace sat down warily.

Wilton aimed the remote at the TV and fired. The old show flashed to life. Faces and voices Grace remembered from early childhood, snow days and sick days spent watching old reruns.

"You see?" Wilton asked. "You thought I was just some boring bookworm or something. But I have my dark side, don't I?"

"Oh, you're something, all right," Grace said, laughing. "You're really something."

*   *   *

The last lip of the sun was dipping below the Allegheny Mountains, rimming the old hills in red and gold as Chelsea and Antonio made their way south from Pittsburgh. Chelsea's artist's eye was fixed on the western sky, which was luminous with the colors of the rainbow. The sweltering summer day had cooled.

They opened all the windows, turned up the radio, and chugged down the interstate. They hadn't seen any sign of civilization for miles. The only thing they could find on the dial were country-and-western stations, and they sang the tunes at the top of their lungs, belting out at the passing trees the twangs and lusty drawls of Patsy Cline and Hank Williams. Chelsea hadn't felt so free and easy in months.

Suddenly, as they were cresting a hill, the engine in her mother's old Dodge Dart coughed. The car lurched, then fell silent. Chelsea and Antonio couldn't do anything except steer the car onto the shoulder and sit there helplessly as they rolled to a stop.

"Out of gas?" Antonio asked hopefully.

"Wishful thinking," Chelsea replied. "We filled up just before we left Pittsburgh."

"Let me take a look under the hood," Antonio said, getting out of the car.

"Wait, you'll get your uniform all dirty," Chelsea said. "Let me."

But Antonio had already unbuttoned his navy dress shirt and thrown it into the car. He popped the hood, then leaned over the engine in his tank top. Chelsea tried not to look, but she couldn't help sneaking glances at Antonio's perfect physique. Every time he moved his arms, another set of muscles she never knew existed rippled beneath his skin.

She knew she had to keep her eyes off him. *Think of it as a test of will,* she told herself. But it was a test she knew she was destined to fail.

"Bad news," Antonio said. "There's stuff busted up all over the place. Snapped fan belt, punctured hoses, leaking oil. It's a miracle we got as far as we did."

"Can you fix it?" Chelsea asked.

Antonio laughed and slapped the dirt off his hands. "If I had the tools and a new fan belt, I could probably get us back to D.C. But the only way to fix this engine is to start over, throw it out."

They squinted over the hill and saw some white buildings and and flat pastures.

They looked at each other and shrugged.

"Lock up the car. And bring that dress with you," Antonio said, smiling. "After all this, I'm not going to take any chances with that thing."

218

It turned out to be a one-of-everything kind of town. One traffic light. One general store. One gas station. One motel.

They kept their eyes off the motel and went for the gas station.

Chelsea pulled her mother's AAA card out of her wallet and dialed the number. She explained the situation, nodded a few times, begged a little, begged some more, then surrendered and hung up the phone.

"Well?" Antonio said.

"Well, nothing. It's late. We're in the middle of nowhere. It'd be an overnight job, anyway. So . . ."

Antonio arched his eyebrows. "You're kidding."

"Afraid not. We're stuck here for the night."

"We could call your parents," Antonio suggested. "B.D. could come get us."

"But what about the car?" Chelsea said.

"I see your point."

They looked toward the motel. Then they looked at each other. They had a hard time hiding their lack of disappointment.

"This is like a scene out of a bad movie," Chelsea said. "But what can we do?"

"After you," Antonio said, gallantly sweeping his arm before him.

They walked over to the motel, entered the office, and rang the bell.

219

"May I help you?" An old woman with gnarled fingers appeared from behind a door marked Private.

"Our car broke down," Chelsea said. "We'll need a room for the night."

"I only have one room," the old woman said, eyeing them suspiciously.

"That's fine," Antonio said quickly, stepping forward with an open wallet. "We're married."

Chelsea gulped but felt herself nodding.

The woman inspected Antonio's clothes. "You in the service?"

"Yes, ma'am. The Naval Academy."

"Well, we're proud to have you with us, then," she said, suddenly brightening. "My husband was in the navy, may he rest in peace. You boys sure did us proud in the Gulf."

"Yes, ma'am. Thank you, ma'am."

"I'll cut down the price a little for ya," the old woman said with a wink.

"Yes, ma'am. Thank you, ma'am," Antonio said, nearly standing at attention.

Chelsea grinned with pride as if Antonio *were* her husband. As if his successes were hers.

The woman pushed the register toward Antonio for him to sign. Antonio's handwriting was impeccable, as always. But Chelsea blushed deeply when she read what he'd written:

Mr. and Mrs. Antonio Palmer, USNA

SIXTEEN

Grace was still humming the *F Troop* song as she pulled into the driveway in front of her house. If she couldn't get it out of her mind, it was definitely going to be a long night.

If you can't get Wilton out of your mind, you mean, Grace thought to herself.

It was funny, but she couldn't seem to stop thinking about him. She guessed it was because he was so different.

And because he's nice, she thought, slamming the car door and skipping all the way to the house. *And he* listens *to me.*

It pleased her that someone so bookish found her interesting and fun to be with.

She threw her keys and her bag onto the couch and was about to turn up the stairs to her room when she saw a shadow pass by the sliding glass door that led to the porch.

"Hello?" she called out. "Carr? Is that you?"

She walked over to the porch and looked out to find Carr in a classic pose of dejection. He was sitting with his elbows on his knees and his head in his hands.

"Why the long face, sailor?" Grace asked.

He sighed softly. "No reason."

"Hmm." Grace nodded, walking over and plopping down next to him. "Soon you'll be trying to sell me Manhattan."

"What?" Carr asked, finally looking up.

"It's an East Coast joke," she explained. "It means I don't believe you."

"Well," he said guiltily, "it's Jody, actually. You know, my girlfriend back home."

Grace nodded, unable to help but notice how the moonlight made Carr's face look even more attractive.

"All the way back home in Kansas," she said.

"Well, she's sort of upset about my coming here," Carr admitted. "Coming east. And I understand, really I do," he went on earnestly. "Lots of people go away and say they'll come back. But lots of them never do."

"And did you say you were going back?" Grace asked.

"I did. And I will." Carr sighed and looked

out at the ocean. "Only she just can't seem to believe me."

"Or trust you, it sounds like," Grace pointed out.

She wasn't sure, but she thought that Carr was blushing again.

"Well," he said slowly, glancing up at Grace quickly and then looking away. "She was kind of upset about you."

"About me?" Grace asked innocently.

"You know, about my . . . living with you. She wanted to know what you looked like."

"And what did you tell her?" Grace asked, perking up.

Carr coughed.

"The whole truth and nothing but the truth?" Grace laughed, feeling pleased and happy enough to let him off the hook.

"She just thinks this place is wild or something. She thinks I'm going to be tempted away by someone."

"Tempted away from your one true love?" Grace asked ironically.

"That's exactly what I told her," Carr replied urgently.

Suddenly Grace realized that Carr's powers of detecting sarcasm weren't nearly as well developed as Wilton's.

"Because, really," Grace continued, testing

her new theory, "what kind of temptation could there possibly be?"

"That's right," Carr replied.

And that's an outright challenge, Mr. Savett, Grace thought, *if ever I heard one.* She smiled and rose. "She'll come around. I'm sure of it."

"Thanks," Carr replied. "Thanks for the support."

Grace made her way upstairs. Once inside her room she went straight for the phone. She quickly dialed a number, and the line rang seven or eight times before someone finally answered.

"Boy, you really sleep like a log," Grace remarked.

"What time is it?" Marta's groggy voice asked.

"Not that late," Grace replied. "I thought you'd want to know right away that you won."

"Won?"

"Cash or check?" Grace asked. "How do you want the ten bucks?"

Grace grimaced as Marta chuckled long and loud.

Chelsea and Antonio stood in the middle of their motel room, looking down at the bed. Outside it was dark. The old woman had drawn the curtains and turned down the bedcovers. *For us to get into bed more easily,* Chelsea thought, suddenly petrified at the thought.

224

"Only one bed," Antonio commented.

"And not a big one, either," Chelsea added.

"Well, how about some TV?" Antonio asked nonchalantly, turning toward the small black and white.

"I think I might take a shower," Chelsea said. "It's been a long day. I still have all that dust from the attic in my hair."

"I know what you mean," Antonio said, brushing the top of his head and laughing a little too loudly.

Chelsea laughed a little too loudly back.

She was so tense, she thought if someone touched her right then, she might shatter into a hundred pieces. She and Antonio were saying exactly what was *not* on their minds, and doing exactly what they didn't want to be doing.

"I think I'll take that shower now," she said mechanically, making a big deal of heading toward the bathroom.

"I think I'll"—Antonio looked around the room for something to do—"sit in this comfy-looking chair," he said, grinning, as if he'd been looking forward to it all day.

"Excellent," Chelsea said, smiling tightly. "I'll just . . . be in here."

She turned for the bathroom as Antonio turned for the chair. They collided in the middle of the carpet. Antonio took hold of her arms.

Their eyes locked. Her lips parted.

Then she pictured him. Connor. Whacking away at his typewriter in Ocean City. Thinner and more haggard by the minute. Chasing his dream. A dream he had shared with Chelsea.

Chelsea pulled away and stepped quickly into the bathroom, leaving Antonio standing empty-handed.

She leaned against the bathroom door and shut her eyes. She loved Connor. She resented him, true. But, still, she loved him. Didn't she?

Chelsea stepped in front of the mirror. "Don't you?" she asked herself.

She undressed slowly, folding everything neatly and leaving it on the sink. Then she studied herself in the mirror again. She knew people called her voluptuous, womanly. She *was* womanly. She would have liked to have been a little thinner, but it was her body, do or die.

Besides, Connor loves it, she thought. He always said so. And, he, her husband, was the only one who should see it this way, right?

She looked at the closed bathroom door. Antonio was just on the other side. A mere few feet away. She could open that door, walk out there and into his arms. She could satisfy her ultimate curiosity: What would it be like with Antonio?

"Isn't that what life is all about?" she asked

226

her reflection. "Satisfying curiosities? Seeking new territory? After all, an artist needs new experiences for inspiration."

It sounded like a good argument. Not an excuse, but a *reason*.

The only reason not to was simple: She had a husband.

As she thought of Connor, the picture she'd had in her mind of her and Antonio made her cringe. It was a mistake, a violation of everything she believed in.

Experience might be a reason, and not an excuse, but it would definitely ruin her marriage. She wouldn't be able to hide it. She knew what a terrible liar she was. She would have to tell Connor, and she knew he'd never forget it. Or forgive it. Their marriage would be over.

And marriage—what was marriage? Maybe she and Connor hadn't figured that out yet, but what they did know was that it was holy. That's what she had grown up believing. And that's what she still believed. It was why she had resisted all the pressure and waited until her wedding night to sleep with a man. Her wedding night with Connor.

I almost rationalized away my entire life, she thought, breathing a sigh of relief and stepping into the shower. She let the water stream down around her, cleansing her, washing away all her thoughts. When she got out, she felt clean and new. She'd scrubbed away all her illicit desire. Nothing bad had happened. She felt strong, ready to face Antonio.

She looked around for her toiletries and realized that she'd left her purse in the other room.

Chelsea opened the bathroom door slowly and peeked her head out. Antonio was seated in the chair, deep in thought.

His head rose as she appeared in the doorway in a cloud of steam, wrapped in a white towel. Her hair hung curly and wild over her bare shoulders. She tiptoed toward her bag, which was lying on the bed.

Antonio's eyes were on her. He stood and walked toward her. The air between them vibrated with electricity. Chelsea giggled nervously. But Antonio's face was set in stone, determined, resolved. As if he'd decided something.

He reached for the corner of Chelsea's towel. He looked into Chelsea's face. She stopped giggling. She was looking away, petrified, not sure what to say or do. And when she didn't move, didn't say no, didn't give any sign of second thoughts, Antonio peeled the towel back.

Justin was waving wildly.

"Allegra, get away from that wheel! You and Kate get the sails down! Now!"

Allegra bounded toward the mast and began working at the ropes and winches. At first Kate didn't move. She was frozen with fear, panic. Too much to do. Were they going to die? Was this it?

"What do I do?" she cried. "What do I do?"

Justin ran up to her and took her firmly by the shoulders. He had a frenzied look in his eye that she'd never seen before. It was anger and fear and sadness and panic all at the same time.

"Kate, listen to me, Kate! Just do exactly what I tell you. No more. No less. I *need* you now. I need you more than ever!"

That snapped Kate out of her stupor. "Okay, tell me what to do," she said.

"Get over there with Allegra and get those sails down!" he said, running back to the wheel. "Now! And make sure Allegra follows my orders."

For a second Kate saw Allegra's and Justin's eyes meet. Justin's were filled with rage, hate. Allegra's with fear. She slunk back, like a scolded child.

The wind and surf were so loud, they had to scream to be heard, racing here and there, working frantically to roll and tie the sails to the boom.

"Get back here with me, Kate!" Justin cried.

Allegra was cowering at Justin's side.

"What did you do to us!" Kate screamed at her.

"I swear, I didn't mean for this to happen," Allegra said.

"What *did* you mean to happen?" Justin shot back.

Then something caught his eye, and he seemed to calm down. Kate thought he actually looked peaceful. She turned her head, expecting to see sudden, miraculous safety. Instead she saw the waves looming above them, growing ever higher, the rocks glistening in the moonlight, so close she could see the mossy algae clinging to their craggy sides.

She looked to Justin for guidance. He was the sailor. He would know what to do. He would protect her. He'd promised her as much. She clung to his arm.

"All right, everybody," Justin said, peering straight ahead. "I want you to listen to me. I want you to reach under here and put on your life preservers. When we get in the water—"

"Get in the water?" Allegra screamed.

"When we get in the water," Justin continued calmly, "we have to stick together. Hold hands and don't let go, no matter what."

Kate was shaking with fear. She saw tears begin to form in Justin's eyes. Allegra began to bawl.

They reached down and put on their orange

floatation devices. Then they faced land. They were getting closer, closer.

"Isn't there anything we can do?" Allegra shrieked.

Kate knew by the look on Justin's face that there wasn't.

"Pray," was all he said.

"I love you, Justin," Kate said.

She felt him squeeze her hand.

"Okay, everyone," Justin said. "Just a few seconds. Hold on—"

But before he could finish his sentence, there was a sickening roar. The boat lurched, throwing all three of them to the deck. Water began spilling over the sides. The boat lurched again, and again, as if someone were kicking it. Kate could hear the beams groan. She thought she heard the snapping of wood.

The twirling undertow and currents spun her like a rag doll. Underwater, she groped frantically. She grabbed hold of something soft, something familiar. She rose to the surface, gulping air. In her hands was Justin's arm. Was he conscious? She couldn't tell. She opened her mouth to scream to him but the water muffled her voice. She couldn't see the boat. She couldn't see any sign of Allegra. Towering waves were shooting up around them like snow-capped mountains, throwing them ever closer toward shore. And the rocks. The roar was deafening.

Kate felt a toothy scrape against her leg. Then total darkness washed over her.

■ HarperPaperbacks *By Mail*

Friends and strangers move into a beach house for an unforgettable summer of passion, conflict, and romance in the hot bestselling series

OCEAN CITY

Look for these new titles in the bestselling *Freshman Dorm* series:

#30 Freshman Temptation

#31 Freshman Fury

Super #4: Freshman Holiday

And in the tradition of *The Vampire Diaries*, now there's

DARK MOON LEGACY by Cynthia Blair.

VOLUME I
The Curse

VOLUME II
The Seduction

VOLUME III
The Rebellion

MAIL TO: Harper Collins Publishers
P.O. Box 588, Dunmore, PA 18512-0588
TELEPHONE: 1-800-331-3716
(Visa and Mastercard holders!)
YES, please send me the following titles:

❑ #1 Ocean City (0-06-106748-2).....................$3.50
❑ #2 Love Shack (0-06-106793-8).....................$3.50
❑ #3 Fireworks (0-06-106794-6).......................$3.50
❑ #4 Boardwalk (0-06-106726-1)......................$3.50

Freshman Dorm
❑ Freshman Temptation (0-06-106166-2).........$3.50
❑ Freshman Fury (0-06-106167-0)....................$3.50
❑ Freshman Holiday (0-06-106170-0)...............$4.50

Dark Moon Legacy
❑ The Curse (0-06-106158-1)............................$3.99
❑ The Seduction (0-06-106151-4)......................$3.99
❑ The Rebellion (0-06-106160-3)......................$3.99

SUBTOTAL..$_____
POSTAGE AND HANDLING*..................$_____ 2.00
SALES TAX (Add applicable state sales tax).......$_____
                            TOTAL................$_____
                            (Remit in U.S. funds. Do not send cash.)

NAME_____
ADDRESS_____
CITY_____
STATE_____ ZIP_____
Allow up to six weeks for delivery. Prices subject to change.
Valid only in U.S. and Canada.
*Free postage/handling if you buy four or more!

☰ HarperPaperbacks *By Mail*

They'd all grown up together on a tiny island. They thought they knew everything about one another. . . . But they're only just beginning to find out the truth.

BOYFRIENDS GIRLFRIENDS

#1 Zoey Fools Around
#2 Jake Finds Out
#3 Nina Won't Tell
#4 Ben's In Love

#5 Claire Gets Caught
#6 What Zoey Saw
#7 Lucas Gets Hurt
#8 Aisha Goes Wild

And don't miss these bestselling *Ocean City* titles by Katherine Applegate:

#1 Ocean City
#2 Love Shack
#3 Fireworks
#4 Boardwalk
#5 Ocean City Reunion
#6 Heat Wave
#7 Bonfire

Look for these new titles in the *Freshman Dorm* series, also from HarperPaperbacks:

Super #6:
Freshman
Beach Party

Super #7:
Freshman
Spirit

Super #8:
Freshman
Noel

MAIL TO: Harper Collins Publishers
P.O. Box 588, Dunmore, PA 18512-0588
TELEPHONE: 1-800-331-3761
(Visa and Mastercard holders!)

YES, please send me the following titles:

Boyfriends and Girlfriends
❏ #1 Zoey Fools Around (0-06-106202-2)........$3.99
❏ #2 Jake Finds Out (0-06-106203-0) $3.99
❏ #3 Nina Won't Tell (0-06-106179-4) $3.99
❏ #4 Ben's In Love (0-06-106183-2) $3.99
❏ #5 Claire Gets Caught (0-06-106187-5) $3.99
❏ #6 What Zoey Saw (0-06-106190-5) $3.99
❏ #7 Lucas Gets Hurt (0-06-106194-8) $3.99
❏ #8 Aisha Goes Wild (0-06-106251-0)...........$3.99

Ocean City
❏ #1 Ocean City (0-06-106748-2)...................$3.50
❏ #2 Love Shack (0-06-106793-8) $3.50
❏ #3 Fireworks (0-06-106794-6) $3.50
❏ #4 Boardwalk (0-06-106726-1) $3.50
❏ #5 Ocean City Reunion (0-06-106233-2) $3.99
❏ #6 Heat Wave (0-06-106234-0)...................$3.99
❏ #7 Bonfire (0-06-106245-6).......................$3.99

SUBTOTAL...$_____
POSTAGE AND HANDLING*.................$____2.00
SALES TAX (Add applicable state sales tax).......$_____
TOTAL..............$_____
(Remit in U.S. funds. Do not send cash.)

NAME_____
ADDRESS_____
CITY_____
STATE_____ ZIP_____
Allow up to six weeks for delivery. Prices subject to change.
Valid only in U.S. and Canada.

*Free postage/handling if you buy four or more!